STEEL TO THE SOUTH

STEEL TO THE SOUTH

Wayne D. Overholser

GUNSMOKE

First published in the UK by Wright and Brown

This hardback edition 2009
by BBC Audiobooks Ltd
by arrangement with
Golden West Literary Agency

ISBN 978 1 405 68270 1

British Library Cataloguing in Publication Data available.

Printed and bound in Great Britain by
CPI Antony Rowe, Chippenham and Eastbourne

Chapter One: KING OF THE DESERT

CLAY BOND RODE WESTWARD across the high Oregon desert, the snowy peaks of the Cascades slowly growing triangles against the sky. He sat slack in the saddle, a lean-jawed man fried down to bone and muscle by a southern sun, the dust of a thousand miles of travel upon him—the red-rock country of eastern Utah, the Wasatch Range, the Great Salt Lake, the twisting passage of the Snake, and now the Oregon desert. He was close to the end of the trail; but he would not reach it tonight, for the sun was showing less than half a circle above the mountain wall to the west, and he was bone-weary.

He had looked at the same monotonous country since early morning, a familiar sight that revived old and nearly dead memories, an empty land of endless miles. He had seen no sign of human life since he had left Harney Valley. Land and sky, the rimrock broken here and there by its age-long struggle with the erosive forces of nature, junipers black dots in the gray landscape, the changeless carpet of sagebrush and bunch grass. It was the same as he had remembered it as a boy except for one ng. Every cow he had seen this day carried the Flying M brand.

Then the sun was entirely gone, and purple twilight flowed across the desert and darkened until the rimrock was a black line below a velvet sky. He topped a rise, and lights made a small cluster below him. Benton's roadhouse, he knew. It was the one place on the trail he would not forget.

It was completely dark when Clay rode into Benton's

yard. The door was open, and lamplight made a yellow splash in front of the house. A hound dog began to bark. Benton called, "Shut up your mouth, Nip," and came out of the house.

Saul Benton, like the desert, had not changed. He had been old and stoop-shouldered fifteen years ago. Now he looked no older. The only difference in him lay in the fact that his shoulders were more stooped than when Clay had last seen him.

"Git down," Benton called. "I've got a bed for you, and supper's still hot. Lava City's thirty miles away."

Clay swung out of the saddle. "I'll take that bed," he said.

For a moment his face was in the lamplight, but Benton did not recognize him. That was the way Clay wanted it and what he had expected. He had been on his way out of the country fifteen years ago. Now, at thirty-one, he bore little resemblance to the kid of sixteen who had spent nearly a week with Benton waiting for his father who never came.

"I'll get your supper set out," Benton said, and swung back into the house.

Clay watered his roan at the log trough and loosened the cinch. He brought him back to the hitch pole, and it was then he heard the thunder of hoofs to the east. If Benton did not know him, it was doubtful if anyone else would. Still, he stepped into the shadows at the corner of the building and waited, right hand wrapped around gun butt. At sixteen he would have kept his place in the light, but the years had bred a caution in him.

There were five of them. They roared into the yard, reining up in the lamplight as if contemptuous of any danger that might be waiting for them. A big man, ponderous of body but not fat, called, "Benton." There was no answer for a moment, and the big man called again, his tone sharpened by impatience, "Benton, where the hell are you?"

Clay did not know the man, but he recognized the type. Heavy lips partially hidden by a bushy mustache, red-veined face, small black eyes sparked by unsubdued violence—this man would be the big poo-paw of the range, and Clay was thinking of the Flying M cattle he'd seen all day.

Benton showed in the doorway, hard-touched by fear and trying not to show it. "Sorry, Bronc. I was back in the kitchen."

"I ain't one to holler twice," the big man said arrogantly. "Who's here?"

Benton clutched the door jamb, fingers long curling claws. "Nobody much. Just a drifter who showed up while ago."

"That his horse?" The cowman motioned toward Clay's roan.

"Yeah, that's his."

"Where is he?"

"Around."

Clay stepped into the fringe of light, his gun riding loosely in leather. He didn't like this man. There was, he thought, someone like him on every range, ruthless and powerful. One quality went with the other. A man of his caliber became powerful because he was ruthless; ruthlessness grew with power. It was an old and familiar pattern in the cattle country where law so often rode with the man who hired the most guns.

"I'm the drifter, friend," Clay said evenly. "Who are you?"

The big man eyed him from dusty Stetson down his lanky body to his scuffed boots. "Bronc Main," he said. "I ask the questions on this range."

"That can change," Clay said.

"Not on the desert." Main laid a thick hand on the saddle horn. "What are you doing here?"

"My business."

The wide face was splashed with red. He moved in the saddle, throwing a quick glance at the rider behind him. He was entirely different from Main, slender and long-fingered, with cold blue eyes. A hired gunhand, Clay thought, and he wondered about it. There had been no one like him on the high Oregon range fifteen years ago. Again he recognized the pattern. Bronc Main and a gun-man would make a natural team. Main had the brains and power and wealth; the gunman was an essential tool to be used when a bank and the law failed Main's greedy pur-pose.

"Proddy," the slender man murmured.

"Let it go," Main said with some reluctance.

"You're smarter'n I figgered." Clay's voice slapped Main.

The cowman lowered his head, passion growing in him. "If you're riding through, we've got no cause for trouble. If you're staying, I'll teach you manners."

"I'm staying," Clay said. "Just made up my mind."

Main stared at Clay, wanting to force the issue, but not certain in his estimate of the man before him. He turned to Benton. "Anybody else here?"

"Nobody."

"Nobody from the Deschutes?"

Benton, still in the doorway, could not keep his gaze from turning toward the interior of the house. He licked thin lips, then blurted, "Nobody."

"Some day I'm gonna catch you lying to me," Main said darkly. "When I do, you're done on this range."

He wheeled his horse out of the lamplight, the rest fol-lowing. For a time the thunder of their going beat into the silence and died. Only then did Benton relax. He said, "Your supper's cold by now, I reckon."

"It'll be all right," Clay said, and moved past Benton into the house.

He ate hungrily, poured another cup of coffee, and canted his chair back against the wall, contentment working through him. He rolled a cigarette, and when Benton came into the room, asked, "Who is this Main?"

Benton began picking up the dishes. "Owns Flying M."

"Big outfit?"

Benton raised his eyes to Clay. "Too damned big. Only outfit in the desert. He's done his share of crowding in the last ten years. Now he's got it all, so he calls himself King of the Desert."

"Who was the skinny gent behind him?"

"Cash Taber. Supposed to be his foreman, but he knows guns better than cows."

Benton limped into the kitchen. Fifteen years ago he had owned one of half a dozen stopping-places between Harney Valley and the Deschutes River, but today Clay had seen no trace of the others.

When Benton came back, Clay said casually, "I was told I'd find five or six places where a man could get a meal, but this is the only one on the road."

Benton stared at Clay as if a gesture or expression reminded him of someone. "You been here before?"

"Once when I was a kid. Seems like I remember other places on the road."

"Ain't been any others for ten years. I've lasted because I don't cross Main. Them that did got moved off. Give a man control of the water holes like Main's got, and you give him the range. Hell of a big country, stranger, and that makes Bronc a hell of a big man."

Clay shrugged and, lowering his chair, rose. "They don't get so big they can't fall."

Benton leaned on the table, a frail old man suddenly turned wistful. He said, "I'm no fighter, but I'd like to see

Main take that fall. It'd be good for the country. He's branching out now, buying land on the Deschutes below Lava City." He picked up the meat platter and then set it down again. "You aiming to make him stumble?"

"I ain't one to go hunting for trouble," Clay said. "Likewise I don't like to be crowded. Main struck me as a gent who's got in the habit of crowding."

"I can't understand why he backed down. Ain't like him."

"I've seen it work that way before. A man rides high on his home range once he gets a tough name, but a name don't mean nothing to a stranger. He figgered it'd be smart to let me find out later he was the big gun hereabouts."

"You said you were staying?"

Clay tossed his cigarette stub into the fireplace. "For a while."

"Bronc's the kind that don't overlook anything," Benton warned. "You'd best keep on riding." He rubbed the back of his long neck, wanting to say more but lacking the courage. Then he blurted, "You ain't a railroad man, are you?"

Clay laughed. "Not me. I've done a little of this and that, but I've missed railroading. Guess this'd be the last place a railroad man would show up, ain't it?"

Benton didn't answer. He stood eyeing Clay, a vague uneasiness working in him. "Damn it, ever since you rode in, I keep thinking I've seen you before. You say you've been through here?"

"A long time ago," Clay said, and went outside.

Chapter Two: THE GIRL IN THE NEXT ROOM

CLAY LED HIS HORSE to the corral and off-saddled. He stood there for a time, smoking, thinking of Bronc Main and Saul Benton. It was no more than a hunch, but the longer he nursed it in his mind, the more certain he became. There was someone in the roadhouse Benton had not wanted Main to find.

He brought his eyes to the second story of the big house. None of the windows were lighted, a fact which proved nothing. He could not forget the way Benton had stood in the doorway, fear gripping him, his eyes turning to the interior of the house. He smoked his cigarette down and threw the stub away, not sure whether this was any of his business or not.

Benton was not around when he returned to the house. A woman came out of the kitchen, saying, "Room five was the one Saul said for you to take."

Clay said, "Thanks," and climbed the stairs.

A bracket lamp spilled a murky light into the hall. He moved along it, looking at the numbers on the doors. He found Number 3. The next door was open, and he heard a woman say, "He wouldn't hurt me, Saul."

Then Benton's voice: "He'd kill a woman as soon as he would a man if he found you snooping. Main's that kind."

They must have heard him then, for they stopped talking. His room was the next one. He went in and lighted the lamp. It was little different from any of a hundred rooms he had seen between the high desert and Utah—the iron bedstead, the straight-backed chair, the pine bureau with its pitcher and washbasin.

He pulled off his boots and gun belt and lay down on the bed, leaving his door open. He had been right about someone being in the house that Benton did not want Main to find. Presently Benton stepped into the hall. He said, "Don't go out there, Vicky. I tell you it's a man's job."

Clay heard the girl's long sigh. "I wouldn't ask a man to do something I'm afraid to do."

"Then let it go. You don't know that Akin's alive. If he's dead, you can't help him."

Benton limped down the hall, the boards squeaking under his weight. The woman's door closed. Still Clay lay there, staring up at the cracked wallpaper, a boy's memories crowding his mind. He pictured the ranch in the canyon of the Deschutes River, the big frame house, the garden and fruit trees, the steady chop of the river as it rolled north to the Columbia, the slanting walls of the canyon. He remembered his mother who had died when he was ten, his father who had taught him about horses and guns and a rope—his father who had dreamed of a big spread but had died before he could turn a dream to reality.

He sat up, built another cigarette, and lighted it. The smoke was bitter on his tongue. He stubbed it out and went to bed, but he did not sleep. There were other memories that held none of the pleasantness of early boyhood, memories long buried that were stirred now by his nearness to his home range.

It had been partly the hard times and the resulting low price of cattle that beat Jim Bond, but mostly it had been Sid Starr who owned the big Triangle S on Buck Creek before it broke down through the canyon wall to the Deschutes. Clay did not remember seeing Starr, but he had heard his father and the one hand, Hungry Hale, talk about him. Starr must have been much the type this Bronc Main was, greedy and arrogant and utterly selfish.

He got up and walked to the window, tension growing in him. He was not a man to ride a thousand miles for revenge. Still, he had come back. He thought, with wry humor, that it would be a good thing if Bronc Main bought north along the river until he came up against Starr's Triangle S. Other memories crowded in, the bitter ones, memories of the things Starr had done because he wanted the Bond ranch on the river. Stolen cattle, burned haystacks, shots from the rimrock. Then Hungry Hale had been badly wounded. Jim Bond had taken him to Prineville, but the sheriff either would not or could not find any evidence against the dry-gulcher.

Then Starr had made his offer to buy, and Jim Bond had beaten him into the dust of Prineville's Main Street; but beating the man had decided nothing. Jim Bond had gone home, knowing he was done. His house had been burned while he and Clay were in Prineville.

"We'll start somewhere else," he said. "You go on to Saul Benton's place. That's off Starr's range. I'll catch up in a day or so."

But Jim Bond never caught up. After six days of waiting the news was brought by a Harney Valley man who had been in Prineville when it happened. Bond had tried his luck with a gun, and it had been bad. Sid Starr had killed him.

Clay went back to bed, restlessness growing in him. Those were the memories he wanted to forget. He had seen men made narrow and vicious by the lust to avenge a wrong. That was not his way, and it was the reason he had not come back before. He had kept up the taxes on the place. He was not a sentimental man; but, thinking about it now, he admitted to himself he had been sentimental in this respect. The quarter section had brought him nothing in return, and it probably never would unless he had the money to put the buildings back and restock it.

A wind had come up, quartering across the desert from the Cascades. It rattled the windows and cried around the eaves. He went to sleep, the wind sounds beating against his ears, but it was not wind sounds that woke him. It was Bronc Main's voice, riding roughshod over Benton. "I'm looking into every room you've got, Saul, and I'll tell you something. If I find that girl, you're finished."

Clay pulled on his pants and boots and buckled his gun belt around him. It was still dark. He felt as if he had not been asleep long, but he didn't risk a match to look at his watch. He made his bed as carefully as he could in the darkness, then stood in the doorway a moment wondering if he had forgotten anything.

He knew nothing about the woman except that he had heard her voice and liked it; but, whether he liked it or not, he wasn't one to sit by while Bronc Main exacted vengeance upon a woman. He slid into the hall, pulling the door shut. Main's angry voice boomed up the stairs, Benton's tired one arguing back. Whatever the connection was between Benton and the woman, it seemed strange that he had found the courage to stand between her and Bronc Main.

Clay tapped on the woman's door. He said, "I'm coming in. I'll handle Main."

The woman said nothing for an instant. Main had begun to curse Benton, his voice raw and wicked. Then Clay heard a blow and killing anger rose in him. It would take a man like Main to hit Saul Benton.

Clay tried the door. It was hooked on the inside. The woman asked, "Who are you?"

"A drifter."

The door swung open. A match burst into flame, the woman holding it high to see Clay's face. For one short moment he saw her, a moment long enough to note three things. She was young, she was pretty, and she was scared.

Men's boots banged on the stairs. Clay shut the door and hooked it, saying, "Get under the bed." He lighted the lamp, took a quick look around the room, picked up a woman's handkerchief, and saw that there was nothing else in sight that would give her presence away. He turned the lamp low. The bed was in the opposite corner of the room. He walked to the door and back to the window, looking at the bed, and was satisfied that the girl could not be seen.

The sound of Main's search came to Clay. Men bawled back and forth across the hall. Then there was a rap on the door. Clay said irritably, "Let me alone. What's the idea making all this racket?"

"Open the door," Main said. "We want to see who's inside."

"That's none of your business."

"Break it down, Alf," Main shouted. "I'll show that hairpin what's my business on this range."

A man's shoulder battered the door open. Bronc Main and another puncher came in and stopped abruptly. Clay stood with his back to the wall beside the window, a cocked gun in his hand. He said, "Show me."

Main looked around the room, black eyes frosty in the lamplight. "All right, Alf. She ain't here."

Main turned toward the door. That would have been the end of it if Clay had not said, "You're sure a tough hand, beating old men like Benton and busting doors in looking for a woman."

Main wheeled back, temper a searing flame in him. "I am tough, friend. You'll find that out if you're here long."

Clay had dropped his gun back into leather. Bronc Main would be tough, he judged, when he held the whip in his hand.

"I'd like to find out now, mister," Clay breathed. "I hate to be wondering about things like that."

The puncher Alf had gone on. The rest of the men were looking through the rooms down the hall. Main stood there alone, breathing hard. Then he wheeled out of the doorway and strode off.

Clay shut the door and slid the chair under the knob.

He said in a low tone, "Better stay there awhile yet, ma'am." He blew out the lamp and waited by the window. The pearl-gray light of dawn was working across the desert, and he could make out the horses in the yard below him.

There was more slamming of doors and futile curses. Then they stomped down the stairs, and Main bawled, "Sorry, Benton. We met old man Shidler on the way to town. He told us she was here, but looks like he had the wrong hunch—which same is damned lucky for you."

They mounted and took the trail to the west. Clay said, "You can come out now, ma'am."

She crawled out from under the bed, a small shapely girl dressed in a man's flannel shirt and Levi's. She said, "Thank you, but you shouldn't have taken a part in my troubles."

"I've got a gift for it," he told her. "Most of my troubles start with somebody else." He moved to the door and paused there, hand on the knob. "You live around here?"

"On a ranch below Lava City," she said. "If you're looking for a job I'll give you one."

"What outfit?"

"Triangle S. It's about thirty miles below town."

Triangle S was Sid Starr's outfit. Clay stood looking at her, remembering that Saul Benton had called her Vicky, that Starr had had a daughter named Vicky. He forced himself to ask the question that was in his mind, "What's your name?"

"Vicky Starr."

"I don't reckon I want that job."

He walked out of the room and down the stairs. He went out into the dawn light, saddled his roan, and took the road to Lava City, a flood of bitter memories washing through his mind.

Chapter Three: VICKY STARR

VICKY STARR HAD LIVED AMONG MEN all her life—cowhands
and freighters and gunmen and saddle bums riding the
grub line. She had learned to judge men, to feel intuitive-
ly that some can be trusted and some cannot. She had
learned, too, that like attracts like. When her father had
been alive, Triangle S had had the toughest crew in the
country; but after his death she had hired Mulehide Cotter to rod the outfit, and Cotter had changed everything
so that now Triangle S bore no resemblance to the spread
that had belonged to Sid Starr.

Standing beside her window, Vicky looked down into
the yard. In the thin light she could not see clearly the
stranger who had defied Bronc Main, but she sensed that
he was saddling up. Presently hoofbeats came to her, and
she knew he had taken the Lava City road.

Her first impulse had been to run down the stairs after
him, to make him tell her who he was and why he had left
so brusquely when he heard her name. There had been a
time when she had been ashamed of the name, when she
had been ashamed of her father and the things he had
believed in. She had both hated and loved him, and more
often than not the hate had outweighed the love; but she
had been young and intolerant. Tolerance had grown
with the years so that she could think of her father with
less bitterness.

Staring into the gathering light, Vicky felt the sharp tug
of anger. Perhaps she owed her life to this lanky stranger;
but he had no call to turn on his heel and walk out simply
because she told him her name. Vicky Starr! Mary Jones!
Sadie Brown! What difference did a name make to some
salty drifter riding through? Well, she wouldn't run after
him. She'd probably never see him again, and Bronc Main

would never see him again; and that was the end of it as far as he was concerned. But it wasn't the end of the trouble between her and Bronc Main.

There was much of Sid Starr in Vicky. She was without the ambition and greed that had consumed him as long as she could remember; but like him she had courage and pride and the passion for doing a dangerous job herself rather than passing it on to someone who worked for her. That passion had brought her into the high desert to try to find George Akin.

She had been wrong in coming here alone, all wrong, and she was touched by humility when she realized the seriousness of the mistake she was about to make. She had known that out here on the high desert Bronc Main recognized no law beyond that which he made himself. Still, she had thought that, being a woman, she could defy Main's orders without running the risks a man would face. But she had underestimated the evil that was in Main, and she had suffered the indignity of being forced to hide under a bed while a stranger saved her life, a stranger who hated the name Starr.

Smoldering anger flamed into fury. She couldn't keep the stranger out of her thoughts. She even resented owing a debt to him, a debt she had tried to repay in the only manner she could. Who did he think he was? Suddenly the fury died. Who was he? Maybe he had a right to hate the name Starr. Plenty of people did. Perhaps he didn't know that Sid Starr was dead, that Triangle S was not what it had been years ago. Saul Benton might know who he was.

Quickly she left the room and ran down the stairs. Benton sat on a leather couch, holding a wadded wet cloth to a bruise on the side of his face. She was instantly contrite, for she had forgotten that he had tried to keep Main from searching the rooms.

She dropped down on the couch beside Benton, asking, "What happened, Saul?"

"Main took a poke at me," he said bitterly. "Knocked me flat. If that drifter hadn't taken chips in the game, Main would have killed me and you, too, I reckon."

"I'm sorry, Saul," she said miserably. "I didn't aim to bring trouble to you by coming here."

He snorted. "No, but you sure aimed to fetch trouble on yourself. I told you what would happen. Wouldn't be so bad if you was sure Akin was alive."

"He must be, or Main wouldn't be afraid to have me nosing around out here."

Benton straightened, his eyes thoughtful. "Hadn't thought of it that way. Don't make no difference, though. You know what'll happen if you go on out to the Flying M."

"I know," she said, "so I'll have to do something else. Saul, do you know who that—that stranger was?"

"No. He didn't give his name, but I keep thinking there's something familiar about him. Like maybe I'd seen him a long time ago when he was a kid."

"Had he ever been here before?"

"Said he had once. Told me he thought there was other places on the road to stop, and seemed surprised that mine was the only one now. I've been trying to think; but for the life of me I can't remember nobody but the Bond boy—"

"Clay Bond," she whispered. "I should have guessed. Hungry Hale wrote for him to come back, but Hungry never heard from him. I've been worrying so much about George Akin that it slipped my mind."

"I reckon that's who he is. I never heard nothing about him after he left here, so I figured he'd cashed in somewhere. I'll never forget the way he sat there at the window." Benton motioned to a chair on the other side of the room. "Then after while he'd go out and just stand there watching the road. A long-legged kid with peach fuzz on his upper lip, his face all screwed up watching for his dad."

Vicky was silent, her face pale. Sid Starr had kept Clay Bond from seeing his father again. She had been only a child at the time of the killing, and she did not remember seeing him before he left the country; but she had heard the story. Of all the people who had suffered at the hands of her father, Clay Bond had suffered the most. She had tried to make amends, but she could not bring his father back to him; she could not give him his lost years. The best she could do was to give his place back to him.

"If he'd known who I was," she said tonelessly, "he'd have stayed out of my trouble; and I can't blame him."

Benton shook his head. "I don't reckon he would have, Vicky. He's considerable man. I never saw nobody face up to Bronc like he done, both when he got here and up there in your room. I didn't see that, but I heard it," he chuckled. "Yes, sir, quite a man. For a while there Bronc didn't even know which end of the stick he was holding."

Vicky rose. "I've got to find him."

Benton stared at her in astonishment. "You're loco. What do you think he's gonna do and say when you ride up?"

"I've got to see him," she said stubbornly. "He doesn't know about the railroad. I can't let him make a mistake."

Benton got up. "Now look here, Vicky. You're as set as a chuckle-headed mule. Bond's the kind who stands on his own two legs, and to hell with everybody else. It's my guess he'd rather make a mistake than be kept from making one by a girl with the name of Starr."

"I've got to try. Anyhow, I'm not going on into the

desert, so I'd better get to Lava City in time for the meeting."

"You ain't et breakfast—"

"I'm not hungry." She moved to the door.

Benton stared truculently at her, then followed, grumbling, "I'm surprised you've got sense enough to quit hunting for George Akin. I was afraid you'd figure this was a good time, Main being in Lava City for the meeting."

She turned. "I guess it would be. I hadn't thought of that."

"Oh, hell!" he groaned. "Why don't I keep my mouth shut? I thought you was going after young Bond."

"I was." She stood motionless, undecided. "I just hadn't thought about Main being gone from the Flying M."

"He wouldn't leave Akin alone," Benton snapped. "You can count on that. Anyhow, if he ain't rubbed Akin out already, there's no reason to think he's going to right away."

"If George isn't dead, it's because Main has some use for him alive; but there's no telling how long he'll have that use for him."

"You've always been a great one for paying debts," he said craftily. "Now I'm asking you who you owe more to, George Akin or young Bond?"

"Well, I—"

"And likewise you're long on trying to wipe out the cussedness your pa did. You've kept up the Bond place so Clay would have something to come back to. Maybe you'd better go tell him."

"I guess that's right," she said, and turned to the door.

Benton masked his face against the grin of triumph that threatened his lips. "I'll help you saddle up," he said, and followed her into the chill pale morning.

Chapter Four: LAVA CITY

THE SUN SHOWED IN THE EAST behind Clay Bond. Daylight flooded the desert, slowly reclaiming the land from shadows. It was very still, the only sign of life the flash of antelopes moving away from the road. The smell of dust was in the air, spiced by the scent of sage crowding the wheel ruts.

He put his horse up a ridge that for a time blotted out the white peaks of the Cascades. Junipers dotted the rocky slopes, gnarled reminders that this was an arid land where only the hardy and tough could survive. Then he topped the ridge, and the green-and-white sky line of the Cascades stood tall against the western sky. He pulled up to look again at a scene he had treasured as a boy. Fifteen drifting years had shown him the West, but nothing else like this.

He stepped down and, building a fire of dead juniper limbs, cooked bacon and made coffee. After he had eaten he rolled a smoke and sat looking at the flat below him, made dark by close-growing junipers. Far to the west a belt of pine stretched from the junipers on to the Cascades. Somewhere in those pines was the new town of Lava City that had grown up since he had left. Beyond was the mountain barrier which separated the high country of central Oregon from the Willamette valley with its lush grass and giant firs and eternal rain.

Clay laid a hand on Colt butt, thinking of what a gun meant and what it stood for in this country of violence and uncontrolled greed, of men like Bronc Main. He wondered about Sid Starr, and why his girl would be threatened by Main. Fifteen years ago no man, even this far from Triangle S range, would have threatened Vicky Starr. He grinned wryly, thinking of the trick Fate had played on him in placing Vicky Starr in the room next to his. Still, he had no regrets. He would have done exactly what he had even if he had known her identity.

Putting the girl out of his mind, he thought about this empty land where life went on unchanged. On the western side of the mountains men lived in security. It was a settled life where law was more than a vague principle to be shifted to suit a man's selfish purpose, where factories belched smoke into the fog and saws screamed as giant logs were laid open, where a railroad lined south to California and steamboats beat the waters of the Columbia and the Willamette into white froth.

He finished his smoke, but still sat motionless, brooding over what had happened, the old injuries fresh in his mind again. He thought of these wasted years when he had found no place that could hold him, no woman with whom he wanted to build a life.

He had learned to use his fists and a gun, necessities for survival in a land like this; but their use had not become an end in itself. He had gone on searching for something he had not been able to define, but he knew he did not want the things so many other men sought. Peace, perhaps, and a fair life where his family and property would be safe from the searching fingers of men like Sid Starr. Like Bronc Main.

The crack of hoofs on rock brought him around, hand lifting gun from leather. He was like a dog in a hostile world, hackles up, waiting to fight. He could have left Bronc Main alone. Instead he had made an enemy. If he stayed, one of them would die. He had no regret on that score, either.

His back trail was shadowed by clashes with men like Main. Sometimes they had died, or he had moved on. Which way it had gone had depended upon circumstances and issues. He had always kept his self-respect because he had his code and he had never varied from it. That was why, as he had told Vicky Starr, most of his troubles had started with someone else.

But it was not Bronc Main or one of his men that rode out of the junipers. It was Vicky Starr. Clay's hand fell away from gun butt, anger working in him. As far as he was concerned, he didn't want to see her again. She rode directly to him, smiling.

"I hoped I'd find you, but you had a start on me." She reined up and stepped down. "Saul said your horse looked like he'd come a long ways, so I thought you wouldn't be pushing him."

"What's the idea of taking out after me?" he asked harshly.

She came toward him, ignoring the rebuff, a slim and supple girl who moved with unconscious grace. She was, he admitted grudgingly, as attractive as any woman he had ever seen. In her early twenties, he guessed, with midnight-black hair that held an unruly curl, and blue eyes so dark they were nearly black. Her lips, full and red and pliant, retained a smile.

"Don't dislike me," she said. "I have my enemies, but it isn't right for a man who saved my life to be one of them."

"I don't reckon I saved your life. I just kept it from being unpleasant."

She shook her head. "Saul Benton says Main would have killed him and me, too. You see, Bronc Main is something less than human. Give a man like that enough power, and take all restraint away from him, and you have a man capable of doing anything."

"Not unless he has reason."

"Main has reason. I think he is holding a man prisoner. Or he may have murdered him. Anyhow, the sheriff pooh-poohs my suspicions. Nobody but Saul Benton believes what I do, and he's too old to fight."

"What were you doing at Benton's?"

"I wanted to go on to the Flying M. I accused Main of murder one day in Lava City and told him I'd get the truth. He laughed it off; then, when he had a chance to see me alone, he told me to stay off the high desert. So," she gestured as if that was proof enough, "I think he's guilty of murder or kidnaping, or he wouldn't have scared like that."

"Murdering a woman is something else," Clay said. "Looks to me like you're spooked."

"Maybe I am, but there is a good deal more to it. Anyhow, I like to pay my debts, and I owe you one. I was hoping I could repay you by giving you a job."

There might be, Clay thought, a sort of justice in what was happening to Triangle S. Benton had said Main was buying land on the Deschutes River. Perhaps Sid Starr was finding himself in the position Jim Bond had been in fifteen years ago.

"I don't need a job. I'll make out."

She frowned, uncertain what to say. "You're a stubborn man, mister. I suppose you'll stay in the country just to show Main he can't buffalo you."

"That might be."

"Then sign on with Triangle S. You'll need an outfit to back you, and I can use a fighting man."

"That's what I thought," Clay said bitterly. "Triangle S is getting pushed, so you think I'll do your fighting. You're plumb wrong, ma'am. I ain't fighting for Triangle S or Sid Starr."

He expected an angry tongue-lashing, but there was none. She said tonelessly, "Sid Starr has been dead for six years, and I don't run Triangle S the way my father ran it."

He stared at her, relief washing through him. He had not come back for revenge. Still, the need to square an old debt had been in his mind through all his drifting years.

He knew he would have killed Starr if he had found the man alive.

"Maybe Starr pushed his luck too far," Clay said.

"Got bucked off a horse." She gave him a straight look. "Saul said you told him you had been through this country a long time ago when you were a boy."

He nodded. "Heard things was about to bust loose, so I thought I'd come back to watch 'em bust." He turned toward his horse and would have mounted.

She gripped his arm. "Hungry Hale is a friend of mine. I was too small to understand what was happening when Jim Bond was killed, but Hungry's told me about it. He said several weeks ago he had written you and asked you to come back."

A sudden tension began working into him. He said, "Well!"

"You're Clay Bond, aren't you?"

"Yeah," he said sourly. "I'm Clay Bond, and I've hung onto the quarter section on the river where our buildings stood. I reckon you've been using it, but it's still mine. Your dad never got his murdering hands on the title."

She flushed, but her voice was expressionless. "I'd like for you to believe one thing, Mr. Bond. I do not see things the way my father did, and I would do anything I could to set things right."

"You'd have to bring Jim Bond back from the grave to do that," he said roughly.

"That's a little beyond my reach, but maybe I can be of some help to you. As for the use of your place, I'll pay you whatever it is worth. I won't try to buy it because you can do better selling a right of way to the Oregon Southern."

"What's that?"

"A railroad," she said impatiently. "It's supposed to be a secret, and some of the rumors flying around aren't true;

but I know for a fact that the Oregon Southern is buying a right of way up the Deschutes to Lava City."

Clay stood looking at her, his mind gripping the implications of what she had just said. This was the reason Saul Benton had asked him if he was a railroad man, the reason Hungry Hale had written that things were about to happen on the Deschutes and it was time for him to come back.

"A railroad means settlers," he said, "and towns and logging camps and sawmills. It means the end of the free range."

"It also means law," the girl cried with unexpected feeling, "and the end of Bronc Main's empire."

He stepped into the saddle, still thinking of this thing she had told him. As a boy he had heard one railroad rumor after another; but they had remained only rumors. The one route, people had said, by which a railroad could reach the high country was to follow the Deschutes canyon, a water grade that pierced the plateau of central Oregon. If it did come that way it would have to climb to the flat above the river, and the lateral canyon carved by Buck Creek would be as good as any. That, then, was the reason his quarter section was worth a fortune, for his land lay in the canyon bottom where Buck Creek flowed into the Deschutes.

"Law is a little slow coming," he said bitterly. "I waited six days for my dad at Benton's, but he didn't show up."

Clay reined his horse toward Lava City, the hard set of his face holding the girl where she was. He did not look back. He followed the narrow road through the junipers, and by noon was in the pines. Half an hour later he reached Lava City and reined up in front of the River Inn.

The place had the marks of a boom town. A wide Main Street paralleled the river a block to the east, the lava dust a thick covering that was constantly shifted by wind and traffic. False-fronted structures crowded the boardwalk, most of them unpainted, the smell of new pine lumber a fragrance in the air. Horses and rigs lined the hitch poles. Men were gathered in knots along the street, most of them farmers, a few cowmen. All were talking, and excitement was a spreading contagion along the street.

Clay left his horse at Royden's stable and had dinner in a restaurant at the end of the block. Then he moved back into the street, and stood gazing on the crowd as he rolled a cigarette and lighted it. He was a long-boned, long-muscled man, pinched in the middle from his years in the saddle, the kind of man who stood out in a crowd, even on this street where other cowmen were gathered. The marks that distinguished all cowhands were upon him, but to a greater degree than most.

Other differences lay deeper than these superficial ones. Life had taken security and comfort from him when he was a boy, had started him drifting. Still, it had not embittered him. He could smile. He could enjoy the small daily pleasures that were his. He retained the capacity to dream, the urge to make that dream reality. It was a dream that had brought him back to the Deschutes, to make his father's ranch the kind of place his father had hoped to have. That had been in his mind through the drifting years in which he had bedded down beside a lonely campfire and lain with his head on his pillow, eyes on a tall, glittering sky.

He finished his smoke and tossed the stub into the dust, his high-boned face holding a grave expression that was close to taciturnity. He was back, he had hung onto his father's quarter section down the river; but now uncertainty like a fog blotted out the trail ahead of him. Change was in the air, tense, brittle, expectant. For the fifteen years he had been away, central Oregon had been an island untouched by time. Now a railroad would wipe out the isolation. What people called progress would come in a high flood.

He saw Vicky Starr ride in, stable her horse at Royden's, and go into the River Inn. Others came into town, and the crowd grew, and the hum of talk became a buzz that worried the air. Bronc Main should be here; but Clay, watching both ends of the street, did not see him. Then, shortly before two o'clock, Cash Taber, the slender man Benton had said was Main's ramrod, made a turn into the street from the east, racked his horse, and disappeared into the Red Crow saloon.

The crowd was flowing into the Red Crow, and Clay moved with it. There were fifty or more men inside, he judged, most of them bellied up against the bar. As the batwings slapped shut behind him he paused, eyes searching the crowd and still failing to find Bronc Main. Even Taber was not in sight.

"Have a drink, friend," a man said. "Seems like everybody's so heated up they haven't got time to be friendly."

He was a medium-tall man, so slender that he seemed frail. At first glance Clay thought he was sick, for his face held a gray paleness. Blue veins lined the backs of his hands. He wore a corduroy suit, cone-peaked hat, and flat-heeled boots, all looking as clean and fresh as if he had just unpacked them.

"Sure," Clay said, and moved to the bar.

"Walt Paddon." The pale man held out a soft hand. "Damnedest burg I ever saw. You can't hear anything but railroad talk. Morning, noon, and night. I came up here for some fishing, but I can't get anybody to go with me."

"I'm Clay Bond. Just got in."

"Clay Bond," Paddon murmured. "Seems like I've heard that name. Wasn't there a Jim Bond in this country years ago?"

"My father." Clay was surprised that he had heard the

name.

"Owned an outfit on the river, didn't he?"

"That's right. Sid Starr shot him."

"That must be why I remember the name. Hasn't been many shootings in this country. What happened to your father's place?"

"I own it," Clay said shortly, uncertain whether Paddon was exercising an idle curiosity, or whether there was a purpose back of his questioning.

"I'm looking for a place to fish." Paddon gulped his drink and set the glass back on the bar. "I want to stay out of doors. I'm not sick, you understand. Just worked too long inside."

Idle curiosity, Clay decided, and he nodded agreement. "Good air here," he said, and waited.

"Maybe we can make a deal," Paddon said eagerly. "There's fish in the river by your place, isn't there?"

"Used to be. Haven't been home lately. Fact is, I left the country when I was sixteen, and this is my first time back. Starr burned our house, so nobody's been living there."

"You're going back, aren't you?"

Clay stared down at the amber liquor in his glass. He had meant to return for years, but it had taken Hungry Hale's letter to bring him back. Now he wasn't sure that seeing what had once been his home would be a good thing. The picture of a smoking pile of ashes was the sharpest of all his boyhood memories. Thinking about it now, he could see no reason to return unless he could make the deal with the Oregon Southern that Vicky Starr had mentioned. He had no money to replace his house and restock the range.

He looked at Paddon, wondering at the eagerness he saw in the man's pale face. "I ain't sure," he said finally.

"I'd make it worth your while," Paddon pressed. "I want somebody who knows the country. To be right truthful, I need somebody to look out for me. I'm the damnedest greenhorn south of the Columbia."

Clay had never been interested in nursing greenhorns. It wasn't his idea of a man's job. Still, if he decided to stay, this could be the means to the end he had in mind, for Paddon looked like money.

"You figger on staying all summer?"

Paddon nodded. "Till bad weather."

Clay opened his mouth to say, "I'll think it over," but he didn't say it. A man poked his head through the batwings, yelled, "Meeting's ready to start," and went on.

Men surged out of the saloon, sudden silence falling upon them.

"Let's go along," Paddon said. "Might be interesting."

"What kind of meeting is it?"

"Something to do with the railroad," Paddon said carelessly. "They've been flocking in from hell-an'-gone to attend it."

Shrugging, Clay said, "All right," and turned toward the batwings.

Chapter Five: THE MEETING

IT WAS THEN AFTER TWO, the sun beginning to drop westward toward the Cascades. Dust rose above the street, stirred by the crowd that had crossed to the lodge hall over the Mercantile. A wind, chilled by its passage across the glaciers of the Three Sisters, rocked the tall pines that crowded the town.

"I've seen a million new towns, I guess," Paddon said thoughtfully. "Most of them look alike, but this burg is different. I don't know what it is. Maybe the river or the mountains. Or maybe it's just the place where they staked out the town, snow peaks on one side and desert on the other."

"What's made it?" Clay asked. "Prineville was the only town around here when I left."

"Irrigation. Some outfit's taken up a lot of land under the Carey Act, and they're building ditches like crazy. You hear the wildest tales about the thousands of people who are going to live here. They must think it's a modern Garden of Eden."

They climbed the outside stairs to the lodge hall, more men crowding behind them. Clay reached the landing and looked down. Vicky Starr was just starting up, a stubby cowhand beside her. Clay followed Paddon inside and stood against the wall, gaze raking the room. There were two groups, the aisle between them, cattlemen on the right, farmers on the left. It had been cow country fifteen years ago. Now the farmers outnumbered the stockmen. The promise of irrigation had brought the settlers in; but whether they would be here in another fifteen years, or even five, was a question in his mind.

Vicky Starr came in and took a seat on the right, the stubby man beside her. Her foreman, Clay thought, noticing he was one of the few in the room who were armed. He would be a fighter, with that square weather-burned face scarred by conflict. Watching him, Clay wondered why she hadn't sent him onto Main's range to find out about the man she thought had been murdered.

A banging in the front of the room swung Clay's attention to the man who stood up there beating a gavel on a table. He had not seen him before, but judged the man was neither cowman nor farmer. He was dressed in a brown broadcloth suit, an elk-tooth charm dangling from a gold watch chain. Clay guessed him to be in the middle thirties, a handsome charming man with a black mustache and white teeth that showed in a ready smile.

"Who's that jasper?" he asked.

"Jason Wade," Paddon answered. "Real estate man.

Owns the townsite. He's been beating the drum for a railroad ever since I've been here."

"All right," Wade was calling, his gavel banging at regular intervals. "Let's quiet down. Do your visiting afterward."

Slowly the hum of talk died.

"Now that's better. I don't know how long Mr. Kyle wants to talk, but the sooner we get him started, the sooner he'll be done; and I know some of you have chores that can't be put off. Gentlemen, and lady," Wade added as if just seeing Vicky in the back of the room, "this afternoon we are finally to have an open answer to what has been a secret."

A laugh swept the room, and his white teeth showed in a pleasant smile.

"At least the railroad people have told us it was a secret. Now that secrecy has been discarded by the Columbia & Cascade Company. Hugh Kyle is here today representing the C. & C.—"

The landing at the head of the stairs squealed under a heavy weight. Heads swiveled toward the door, and Wade stopped talking. There was that moment of silence, and then Bronc Main, as if timing his entrance for this dramatic moment, walked in, Cash Taber behind him.

"Couple of chairs in front, Bronc," Wade called. "Glad you're here. Some of us were wondering what had delayed you."

"Thanks, Jason," Main boomed, and strode up the aisle, Taber trotting behind him.

"Now," Wade went on, "I was just saying that Hugh Kyle is here to lay his cards on the table. Face up. Without taking any more of your time, I'll present Mr. Kyle." He nodded at a man sitting in the front row. "The floor is yours, Hugh."

Kyle rose to the roar of clapping hands and feet banging on the floor. There were whistles, and some of the farmers were on their feet shouting, "Hurrah for Kyle."

"Damned fools," Paddon breathed in Clay's ear. "The C. & C. will never build into this country. They've been forced to make a show because the Oregon Southern is moving in, but they won't do anything except try to hold the O. S. out."

Clay didn't understand, but he nodded, eyes on Kyle. He was about forty, Clay judged, the kind of man who would fit into a new country. Medium-tall and blocky, he had a stubborn jaw and the sun-bronzed skin of one who has spent the most of his waking hours out of doors.

"Thank you, Jason," Kyle said, nodding at the chairman. He leaned across the table, big fists pressed against it, flinty eyes making a slow study of the crowd. "You've been told why I'm here. The time for talk and idle rumor is past. The time for action is here."

The settlers cheered him again, wildly and spontaneously, but there was little response from the right side of the room. That, Clay knew, was to be expected. A railroad meant little to stockmen; it was an essential to farmers.

Kyle held up his hand. "Boys, I'll get down to brass tacks. I can't promise you how soon you'll hear a locomotive's whistle in Lava City, but I can promise you this. You'll hear that whistle as soon as it is humanly possible to lay steel south of the Columbia, and we'll start laying that steel the instant the preliminaries are done. We've heard a lot of talk lately about how badly this country needs a railroad, about it being the biggest untapped area in the United States where primitive methods of the old frontier are still the means of moving products. We've heard about the riches of central Oregon—thousands of acres waiting for the plow, the finest stand of yellow pine in the country waiting to be logged. Gentlemen, the Columbia & Cascade is about to tap that treasure chest."

They cheered him again, even Bronc Main stomping and clapping. Slowly and a little doubtfully the rest of the stockmen followed Main's lead. Kyle smiled and raised his hand again.

"Now let's get down to the real business at hand. As you know, railroad building is a terrific gamble. Construction of this line will be particularly expensive and difficult because of the terrain. We must follow the Deschutes canyon for miles. That means rock work. Tunnels. Bridges. Tremendous difficulties in getting men and supplies into the canyon. It is only fair that you who will profit by this road should help bear the burden. That's why I'm here. My people have given me one definite order."

Kyle paused, sober face turning as his gaze bored into the eyes of every man in the room. There was a moment of silence when even the breathing of more than a hundred people seemed to stop. Then he said, "My order was to determine how anxious the people of central Oregon are to have this railroad."

"We're mighty damned anxious," a settler bawled. "What do you want of us, Kyle?"

"We want you people to furnish us with a right of way from here to the Columbia."

They stared at him, stunned. The farmers had no money, and stockmen like Bronc Main didn't care one way or the other.

"That's the way the C. & C. operates," Paddon whispered. "Throw their failure to build into the laps of the people."

Jason Wade was staring at Kyle as if this was the last thing he had expected to hear. He said, "Hugh, just offhand I'd say the right of way would cost a hundred thousand dollars, and we don't have that kind of money."

"All right. Say a hundred thousand. What do you think laying steel up here will cost us?"

"I don't know—" Wade began.

"I don't either, but it will be millions. Not thousands." Kyle reached for his hat and turned to the audience. "Boys, I know that's a big chore to drop into your laps. Think it over. If you decide to go ahead, select one of you to buy the right of way. Then communicate with me in Portland. When your end is attended to, I'll get busy on mine."

"You're in no rush," Wade said. "Your stage doesn't leave till night."

"I thought you'd rather talk it over without me being here."

Wade shook his head. "It won't hurt you to hear what we've got to say. I believe I stand to profit as much by this railroad as any man in the room, but I can't put up any big part of a hundred thousand dollars." He swung to the audience, stepping in front of Kyle. "There is another chance, boys. Let's contact the Oregon Southern. I've heard rumors that they're interested in this country."

Kyle laughed. "Go ahead, Wade—contact the Oregon Southern. But you know that outfit is owned by a couple of Portland promoters who don't have anything but some paper and a few stakes. It takes money and savvy to build railroads, and we've got it. The Oregon Southern hasn't."

Bronc Main reared up to his feet. "Kyle's right, Wade. It don't make a hell of a lot of difference to me. My cows can walk to the Columbia." He waved a beefy hand toward the farmers. "These boys are different. You don't walk hay and potatoes and hogs to market. Looks to me like we'd better do business with the man who's on the ground. I'm just looking at it from the standpoint of the whole country, 'cause it's like I say. I don't give a damn for myself."

The farmers eyed Main, suspicion plain to read on their weather-burned faces. They knew him for what he was. Some of them had tried to homestead on the high desert and had been driven off by his riders. They knew, too, that he was buying land on the river below Lava City, and that meant the Flying M was spreading out.

"This is mighty generous of you, Mr. Main," Kyle said, "but you'll find that a railroad will mean more to you than you think."

Main shrugged, heavy lips curled into a sardonic grin. "Maybe, Kyle, but I figger it'll do me more harm than good. I do know one thing. It'll bring sodbusters in by the thousand. That means trouble for me."

"You say you want to do business while Kyle is here," Wade cut in. "Just how do you propose to do that?"

"He can leave us some blanks," Main said, "and we'll get somebody to sign up the right of way." His black eyes ranged over the crowd. "Lew Dagget'll do. He lives down the river, and he can see everybody easy. Then the C. & C. will hold an option on the right of way. They'll know where they stand. After we do that, we'll go at the money-raising job. Or we can pledge it here." He stuck his hands into his coat pockets. "I'll give a thousand dollars to start things off."

The burly man he had called Lew Dagget got to his feet. "I'll give five hundred and donate my time. Fact is, I'll donate the right of way across my land."

"Now you've got the proper notion," Kyle said approvingly. "I don't see that the right of way should cost any big money, Wade. The men on the river who own land will find their property doubled or tripled in value by the railroad. Why shouldn't they donate it?"

"Because the value of the land on the lower river will not be doubled or tripled," Wade said. "It's different up here. This country has to have a railroad if it ever amounts to anything, but there's nothing in the lower canyon that ever can be developed except some potential dam sites."

"It's a wheat country," Main said hotly. "What the hell

are you talking about, Wade? You ought to go down there and take a look—"

"Maybe you never heard of the branch line that comes as far south as Triumph," Wade cut in. "Wheat and sheep go out on that line. When you've said that, you've said it all as far as that country goes."

Paddon had been muttering something Clay couldn't catch. Now he stepped over to Vicky Starr and whispered to her. He came back, pale face dark with suppressed fury. He breathed, "The damned fools. The crazy damned fools. They can't see as far as the end of their noses."

Vicky was on her feet, a slight straight figure. She called, "Jason, may I say something?"

"Of course," Wade said. "Most of you boys know Vicky Starr. Her Triangle S is one of the biggest outfits between here and the Columbia. If anybody in this meeting knows what's going on, it's Vicky."

They turned to look at her. Bronc Main kept his feet for a moment, big face mirroring his resentment. Clay, watching this shift in the run of events, sensed that Main had been on the verge of putting over his program. Now, with Vicky's first words, his chance was lost.

"I do know what's going on," Vicky said clearly, "because a railroad has been my pet hope for years. Last winter I went back to St. Paul and Chicago, where I talked to the big men in the business, not little fry like our friend Kyle. That's why I can make one flat statement I hope you will believe. Kyle will deny it, but I know it's true." She gave him a straight look, her lips curling in scorn. "The Columbia & Cascade will never build to Lava City unless forced to by the Oregon Southern."

There was a moment of silence. They sat turned in their seats, cattlemen and farmers, staring at her as if stunned by what she had said. Then Kyle laughed shortly. "Boys, she's right on one thing. I will deny that statement. If a man said it, I'd know what to do, but I'm puzzled when a woman mixes in men's business."

"It's natural he would deny it," Vicky said hotly, "because we're pawns in a game that is bigger than any of you guess. We are led to believe that the Columbia & Cascade and the Oregon Southern are local companies designed to deal with a local situation. The truth of the matter is that major transcontinental lines are behind both of them. Kyle's bosses now virtually control railroad transportation in Oregon. The Oregon Southern people want a share of that business. If you men give them the help they need, and it will not be financial like Kyle asked for, the Oregon Southern will start building before the summer is over. Why? Because a line east of the Cascades running south to San Francisco will reach into the real treasure box of the West. Don't think for a minute that central Oregon is the end in itself. We're just a whistle stop on what will be a main line."

Still they stared, hardly breathing. Some were frankly puzzled, too ignorant of Oregon geography and the growing tension in the railroad world to understand. Others, including Jason Wade, were thinking in new and bigger terms than they ever had thought before.

"Well, boys," Kyle said sourly, "I'll run along. My proposition stands. If you want to listen to a woman that's your privilege; but if you wait for a two-bit outfit like the Oregon Southern to lay steel to Lava City you'll have quite a wait."

He started for the door, a sour and angry man. Burly Lew Dagget was on his feet, bawling, "Hold on, Kyle. Who said we was listening to a woman? She's a neighbor of mine. I know how much you can believe of what she says."

Lew Dagget was a cattleman. Clay remembered the name, although he could not identify the man or his outfit. Now, staring at his leather-brown face, twisted by the fury that was growing in him, he saw the man in the same light he saw Bronc Main, greedy and ruthless and entirely selfish. But Daggett was worse than that. Even Main had not been capable of saying publicly what he felt about Vicky Starr. Dagget had, and that was enough to bring Clay away from the wall.

"Dagget," Clay said coldly. "Come out here."

Dagget's yellow eyes, turned cautious now as he looked at Clay, lost some of their belligerence. "Why?"

Bronc Main was on his feet, shaking a fist at Wade. "Look here, Wade. You told me this meeting was for landowners."

"It is," Wade said. "I don't know who this fellow is."

"A saddle bum," Main roared. "A gunslick saddle bum riding through the country. I say to throw him out, and we'll get on with our business."

"You want to do the throwing?" Clay asked.

He stood alone in the back of the room, his eyes gray flint under arching black brows. He was not, judged by his appearance and the gun holstered within inches of his right hand, a man to be taken lightly.

"This is no place for brawls," Wade cried frantically.

No one paid him any attention. The farmers were watching, wanting no part of this. The cowmen, most of them in line of fire, were edging away. Hugh Kyle slipped a hand inside his coat. Only Walt Paddon, still standing against the wall, was smiling as if he enjoyed this drama that was being played out before him.

Bronc Main, caught between Clay's challenge and his pride, could find no escape. It was his foreman, Cash Taber, who stood up and gave Main the solution he sought.

"Strikes me, Wade," Taber said crisply, "that this saddle bum has no place in the meeting." He pointed a slim finger at Dagget. "Neither has he. I say the lady has a right to speak her piece, right or wrong, but Lew was out of line."

"That's right," Wade said quickly. "Get out, both of you, and we'll get on with the meeting."

"It's gonna be quite a chore throwing me out," Clay said. "I've got more right here than most of you. The railroad will run through my place, whichever outfit builds it."

"Your place?" Wade studied him, trying to recognize him and failing. "What place do you own?"

"The Bond ranch on the river," Clay said shortly.

Bronc Main let out a gusty breath. He muttered, "Clay Bond," a sudden interest showing in his black eyes.

Kyle's gaze was fixed on Clay. "I guess you've got all the right in the world to be here, Bond. As a matter of fact, I'm glad to see you. Your quarter section has worried us. We didn't know where to find you. You're very right when you say any railroad coming up the canyon will cross your land. The west wall at that particular point is too steep to be considered."

"We're getting off the point," Clay said, his voice honed sharp by the prodding anger that was in him. "Miss Starr sounded like she knew what she was talking about. I don't know what you boys think, but I say Dagget's got a coat of tar and feathers coming."

"You're damned right," a farmer yelled. "Let's give it to him."

The settlers and most of the cowmen began moving toward Dagget, not hearing Wade's frantic shout. "No trouble now. Let's have order."

Dagget licked thick lips. A hand came up to his face, fingers touching a great strawberry splotch that disfigured his right cheek. He threw a quick glance at Bronc Main and found no support there. He mumbled, "All right. Get on with your meeting." He rammed into the aisle and hurried toward the door.

Clay said, "You're apologizing, Dagget."

The burly man hunched his shoulders, hands fisting. "Like hell I will—"

Then a surprising thing happened. Cash Taber moved in behind him, gun muzzle prodding his back. "You were out of line, Lew. Apologize to the lady."

"Sorry, ma'am." Dagget's tongue tip swept over dry lips again. "I got no reason to doubt what you say."

"For once you're telling the truth," Vicky Starr said; "but you're saying this because you're forced to. Our trouble will be settled later."

As Dagget stumbled past her and left the room Clay's eyes locked with Taber's. He said, "Friend, I misjudged you. You're smart."

Taber grinned, drawing a pleasant mask over his sharp-featured face. He said softly, "Thanks. You're a little ahead of me. I haven't figgered out how smart you are."

He swung back to his seat. Clay moved to the wall again. The rest sat down, but the atmosphere was not one favoring the consideration of more business that day. Wade, understanding that, lifted his gavel and said, "We'd better adjourn the meeting—"

"Wait, Jason," Vicky called. "You men can believe me or not, but please do one thing. Talk to the Oregon Southern man before you sign up with Kyle."

"They haven't got a man in here," Wade said wildly. "We can't do anything more today."

"There's a great deal you can do today." Walt Paddon strode down the aisle. Swinging to face the crowd, he said, "I represent the Oregon Southern. I had not expected to make my identity known at this time, but the meeting has forced me. Gentlemen, the Oregon Southern, as Miss Starr told you, is not owned by two Portland promoters as Hugh Kyle would have you believe. The best railroad savvy in the country is behind it, and we've got all the

money we need to build as far south as we deem necessary."

Kyle was staring at him. He breathed, "Paddon, I didn't
recognize you, standing back there."

"I've been around, Hugh." Paddon held out his hand.
"Been quite a while since we met. This will be another
fight. That's a promise."

Kyle shook his hand and dropped it. He said, "Boys,
you'll have a railroad sooner than you expected. Maybe
two. My offer stands, regardless of what the Oregon Southern does."

"Some of you have already signed right-of-way agreements with us," Paddon said crisply. "I'm ready to do
business with anyone who has not signed, and I want to
make one point clear. We are not asking for anything
free. We'll pay cash the instant you sign the agreement."

Kyle, glaring at him, bawled, "So will the Columbia &
Cascade."

Wade put a shaking hand to his head. "Two railroads,
and here we've been all this time without any." He pounded his gavel. "It's up to the railroad representatives now.
Meeting adjourned."

Chapter Six: DECISION

MEN MOVED OUT OF THEIR SEATS, jostling and shoving and
swearing in their anxiety to reach Kyle and Paddon. Clay
left the room and went down the stairs, eyes raking the
street for Lew Dagget. There was much he didn't know;
but it seemed a fair guess, from the way Main had named
Dagget as the man to get the agreements signed up, that
a deal had been made before the meeting to support
Kyle's proposals. Whether that was true or not, he was
sure of one thing. By supporting Vicky Starr he had made
another enemy.

"Clay!" Vicky was coming down the stairs behind him. "Wait, Clay."

He had reached the street when he heard her. Then he saw Dagget in front of the Red Crow, and knew that trouble was here.

"Clay, wait."

He swung back, irritated. "I seem to be backing your play, but don't think I'll keep it up."

"I know," she breathed. "There was nothing personal in what you just did. Defending womanhood in general, but not me in particular."

Clay, watching Dagget, saw that the big man had moved into the street. "That's it. I ain't one to forget your last name is Starr."

Her chin was high. "I can't help what my last name is, but at least I'll thank you for what you did this morning. You were magnificent."

He swallowed. He liked hearing what she had just said. For a moment he forgot Lew Dagget. Vicky Starr, pretty and desirable, stood within his reach, liking him and wanting him to like her.

He wiped a hand across his forehead. "I respect anybody who stands up for what he believes in, man or woman." He swallowed. "I never saw a woman who had that kind of courage before. It was—kind of magnificent."

"Coming from you," she said, "that's a real compliment. Are you going to your place now?"

He held his answer a moment, thinking of Paddon. The fishing trip would probably be off now if the railroad man had wanted it to cloak his real activities. He said, "I don't think so."

"Fifteen years can change a lot of things, Clay."

"It can't change some things," he flung back. "Geography is one of them. Triangle S is on one side of me and the river's on the other. No matter what I did, I'd never have more than a ten-cow spread."

"I'd let you through to the open range. I'll sign an agreement to that effect. If Triangle S can do anything for you—"

"Bond," Dagget called, "get away from the woman."

Clay said thickly, "Triangle S has done enough for me. Get off the street." And he turned to face Lew Dagget.

He had seen such men, soured by life and ruled by bitter passion. Pride was Dagget's one slim hold on self-respect, and his pride had been injured. He was moving now to bolster it in the one way he could.

"I'm gonna bust you up, sonny," he called. "I'll fix that face so it won't ever be the same." Apparently he was not carrying a gun.

Clay stood motionless, watching the big man come on, great arms swinging at his sides, thick shoulders thrown forward, a wicked grin of anticipation on his lips. Weight and strength were Dagget's advantages, surprise would be Clay's if he played it right.

Clay stood in the street dust, making no move to either advance or run. Dagget, sensing uncertainty in him, came on, mouth pulled wide by his grin. The wind had died down. The sun, untouched by cloud or haze, laid a hard shine upon the street. Dust stirred under his boots. He brought his hands up in front of him, fingers spread.

"You made a mistake up there, sonny," he breathed.

He expected Clay to break and run; or, at the worst, to retreat and stay out of reach. There would be no mercy, once he had the slim body in his grip. Clay, eyes pinned on the big man's muscle-ridged face, read his intent; but he sensed, too, the plodding quality of Dagget's mind. Expecting one thing, he would be slow to react to anything else. So Clay stood waiting it out until Dagget's huge hands were almost on him. Then, timing his forward motion to the exact instant, he exploded, right fist hitting Dagget on the side of the head with a crack that ran across the silent street in meaty echoes.

Dagget had been hungering for the fight. It was there in his yellow eyes, in the shallow lip smile. Still, he was not prepared for what Clay did. Nobody on the Deschutes had risked a fight with him for years, and his reputation had spread up and down the river. Surprised and partly stunned by the blow, he fell and rolled over in the dust. He came to his feet and shook himself, letting out a great bawl of rage.

Clay was on him, battering him with both fists and forcing him back. Blood spewed from his nose. He clubbed Clay with his arms, trying to protect his face. Then Clay hammered him in the stomach, driving air out of him in gusty sighs. He fought for breath, making a stand and taking Clay's blows and beating back with fists that jarred and hurt; but Clay had made his plan and didn't compromise with it. The only chance he had was to keep Dagget from becoming the aggressor.

Again Dagget retreated, blowing and cursing, blood a steady flow from his nose. Clay gave him no rest, hitting him first in the face and then the middle. The big man's face showed his hurt. He fell a second time and rolled over and turned on his back, a gun in his hand.

It was a final act of desperation. Clay jumped on him, high boot heel grinding into the flesh of Dagget's wrist. He howled in pain, relaxing his grip on the gun butt. Clay kicked the Colt away. He said contemptuously, "Get up."

Dagget rose, a lumbering effort like that of a shaggy dog, beaten until his self-respect had gone out of him. Dust on his face made a bloody drooling mask of mud. He came on, slowly and doggedly, jabbed a thumb at Clay's right eye, missed, and tried to knee him. Clay turned his body. Dagget missed again and was momentarily off balance. Clay caught him with a short up-swinging right on the point of the chin. He went down in a cumbersome fall, and dust rose around him, and he lay still.

Clay stepped back and sleeved sweat from his face. Turning, he was aware of the crowd that had come out of the lodge hall and spilled into a long line at the side of the street. Vicky Starr was still there; the stubby man who had come in with her; Bronc Main, disappointment showing through his attempt to hide it; Cash Taber, sizing Clay up as coolly as a beef buyer sizes up a fat steer; Hugh Kyle and Walt Paddon and Jason Wade and the rest of them.

Clay said, "Dagget got any friends in the crowd?"

"I'm his friend," Bronc Main said, "but I don't do his fighting for him. Just one thing, Bond. Lew's got a hell of a good memory, and I don't ever remember seeing him licked before."

"He's been licked now." Clay pinned his gaze on Paddon. "If that fishing trip's off, I'll be riding."

"Who said it was off?" Paddon cried. "I'm done here. I'll ride along."

For a moment Clay's eyes were on Vicky Starr. She was pale and a little worried, and when Clay turned toward his horse she left the crowd and fell into step beside him.

"It was a good show to most of them," she said, "but I know how much more it was. Clay, don't hate me. We've got a job to do together."

He ran a sleeve across his face again, aware only then that Dagget's clubbing fists had hit more than once during the fight. He said sourly, "You sure keep trying."

"I know," she said a little apologetically. "I wouldn't if you were any other man, but you're Clay Bond. You've given me a hand twice. You were forced into that fight because of what you did for me, but there's more to it than that. Clay, you and I hold the future of the railroad in our hands."

He had reached his horse. He stopped, looking down at the girl, puzzled. "How do you figger?"

"I said in the meeting that the C. & C. would not build unless forced to by the Oregon Southern. What happened today will force Kyle to do something. He'll use money for his weapon."

Clay saw how that could be. He asked, "Sure, but what's that got to do with me?"

She started to say something and then decided against it.

Hugh Kyle had come up behind them. Ignoring Vicky, he said, "That was a hell of a good fight, Bond. Plenty of Dagget money up when it started, but no takers." He shook his head ruefully. "I had a hunch, but I wasn't smart enough to play it."

Paddon called from across the street, "I've got a horse in the stable, Bond. I'll be with you as soon as I get my stuff out of the hotel."

Kyle chewed his lip, trying to hold his good humor. "Bond, you stumbled into something when you rode back just at this time. I made a mistake when I didn't find out Paddon was on the ground. Maybe you know how these things go. You don't give any more than you have to, but when the chips are down you fight like hell. Crazy for two railroads to build up the canyon, but it looks like that's what'll happen." He paused, grinning ruefully. "Unless one of us can stop the other one."

"In which case you won't build at all if you can stop the Oregon Southern," Vicky cried. "Don't beat around the bush, Kyle. You can sit tight and save the cost of building a railroad up the canyon because if we go on using horses and wagons to freight our stuff to Triumph, your two-bit branch line will go on getting the business."

Kyle appeared to notice her for the first time. "I make it a rule never to argue with a lady," he said courteously, "but there is one thing I don't understand. Most of the stockmen are on our side. Why aren't you?"

"Because the country needs a railroad," she answered quickly. "I'm backing the line that I know will build."

"You don't know we won't build."

"You're wrong, Kyle. The top men in your company told me flatly they weren't interested in building unless the competition forced them to. It's like I just said. Your company is getting the business now because we have to freight our stuff to your railhead at Triumph."

Kyle shrugged. "Paddon's signed you, I suppose. It's unfortunate I didn't get there first. I could have topped his offer."

She gave Clay a direct look. "I told you."

"A dollar is a dollar," Clay said, "no matter whether it comes from the Oregon Southern or the C. & C."

"That's right," Kyle agreed, "and we might as well get your name on the dotted line right now." He reached into his pocket for a form. "Name your price, Bond."

"This is more than a dollar," Vicky cried. "If you sell to Kyle, you'll be deciding what will happen in central Oregon for the next fifty years."

"Name your price, Bond," Kyle repeated.

"You seem to have more money than you did in the meeting," Clay murmured. "You were talking about us donating the right of way, or buying it ourselves."

Kyle grinned. "You don't expect a railroad company to pay for something it can get the other fellow to pay for, do you? I said name your price."

"One hundred thousand dollars."

"The hell. Is that your price to Paddon, too?"

"I'm not talking to Paddon."

Kyle wheeled on Vicky. "This is your round, ma'am,

but there's a few more coming. I think you'll regret winning this one." He stalked away, heels cracking against the boardwalk, a furiously angry man.

Vicky looked at Clay, her dark eyes shining, her full lips lightly pressed. She said softly, "We fight for the things we believe in, Clay. After you've been back long enough to see what's happening, you'll believe in the things I do." She started to turn away and then faced him again. "I want to be a neighbor. Don't let your hate for the name Starr make you blind."

She walked away, as graceful and supple as a young pine. His eyes were still on her when Walt Paddon rode up. Aware of his presence, Clay raised his head. "What did you do to get her on your side?"

Paddon didn't answer for a moment. He laid his gaze on Clay as if weighing him in the balances of his mind. Then he said, "I take it you didn't sell to Kyle?"

"No. I asked you a question, Paddon."

"I know, but I doubt if you will believe my answer. I didn't do anything. She has sold us the right of way through her place. Her price was one dollar." Paddon shifted his weight in the saddle, his forehead creased by a thoughtful frown. "Bond, there is something in Vicky Starr that I have never found in another person, a sense of responsibility for her father's greed."

"You still haven't answered my question."

"I gave you the answer, my friend. She's the reason I'm out here. If she hadn't described this country to my superiors, I doubt that we would ever have bought the Oregon Southern from the Portland promoters Kyle mentioned. You see, she knows how much a railroad is needed, and she's damned sure we'll build one."

Clay painfully pulled himself into the saddle. He looked back along the street. Dagget was gone. Neither Bronc Main nor Cash Taber was in sight. He thought of Kyle and his relationship to Main, of what Kyle had said to Vicky.

Clay Bond had never run away from a fight in his life. He would not run from this one. Vicky's last name might be Starr; he did not believe in all the things that she did, but he would be here at the finish. Circumstances had pitched him into the fight, but it was his decision that would keep him in it.

Chapter Seven: CONFERENCE

Hugh Kyle stood in front of the hotel and watched Clay Bond and Walt Paddon ride out of town. Bond looked as if he belonged in the saddle, but Paddon rode awkwardly in the manner of a man to whom a horse is a stranger, and who hates every second he is in leather. It was, Kyle knew, a piece of play-acting on his part. By the time they were out of sight, he would be riding with the same ease and grace that characterized Bond.

Slowly the anger died that his failure with Bond had aroused in him, for he was never a man to be possessed by any great emotion. He was a coldly logical machine continually driving toward one objective, and he seldom permitted himself to be sidetracked from the pursuit of that objective. The meeting had not gone as he had expected, and Bond had played cute when he had been offered a deal for the right of way across his property. That was understandable, for it simply marked him as a shrewd businessman who wanted to make the most from an advantageous position.

The danger was that Paddon might talk him into signing, for the girl was on Paddon's side. That was a complication Kyle didn't like. It had been his experience that money always spoke a language men understood, but that women spoke quite another language, and all too often, when they were as pretty as Vicky Starr, their talk rose above the rustle of greenbacks.

For several minutes Kyle remained motionless, eyes on Paddon and Bond until they disappeared into the pines north of town. He lifted a cigar from his coat pocket, bit off the end, and lighted it, his machinelike mind searching for some weapon that would balance his hand against Paddon's. A show of force might do. He made the decision and turned into the Red Crow.

The farmers had left town; but the cattlemen had remained, and the saloon was crowded with them. Bronc Main was there, bellied up against the bar beside Lew Dagget, whose battered face was as raw as a side of freshly butchered beef. Cash Taber stood at the end of the bar by himself.

Kyle was a keen judge of men, and he understood the gunman. Taber belonged with the cowmen, yet he was not a part of them. He was supposed to be the Flying M foreman, but in reality Main had no foreman. Taber was a hired gun slinger, no more, no less. Now he stood with a filled glass before him, absently turning it with the tips of his fingers while he listened to the talk, a thin smile on his lips as if he were a spectator to this scene rather than a participant.

Moving in beside him, Kyle said, "I'll buy you a drink, Cash."

The gunman shook his head. "Thanks, but this one's gonna do me. Dagget can get drunk to forget what Bond done to him, but a man in my position has got to go easy on whisky."

"You're smart." Kyle motioned to the bartender and dropped a coin on the mahogany. "Good fight."

"A hell of a good fight," Taber agreed. "I don't know how you size Bond up, but from where I stand he looks like a pretty tough customer."

Kyle took his drink and set the glass back. "With his fists anyhow."

Taber laughed softly. "You think maybe he ain't so good with his gun? I've been wondering about that, too, and I reckon I'll keep on wondering till I find out."

Kyle nodded, understanding. A stranger who made the splash Clay Bond had, always presented a challenge to a gunman like Taber—a challenge so strong that he would not rest until the test had been made.

"Don't be in too much of a hurry about finding out," Kyle said. "Not till he signs a right-of-way agreement with me."

Taber's sharp-featured face held an expression of cat-like cruelty. "Sure. I'm willing to wait. For a day or so."

"Make that a week," Kyle said curtly. "It may take a little doing. I'm going to my hotel room. Fetch Main up. I want to see him."

Taber nodded. "We'll be along."

Kyle left the saloon and, going back to the hotel, picked up his key and climbed the stairs. The smell of new pine lumber lingered in the narrow inclosure of the hall. The same smell was in his room, for the hotel had been open only a few days.

A sharp dislike for his kind of living filled him as he closed the door behind him, his eyes sweeping the room with its crude furniture. There was a pine bedstead with a cheap lumpy mattress, an unpainted bureau with its tall white pitcher and washbasin, and a single rawhide-bottom chair. Even the mirror above the bureau was typical of the rest of the furniture. When he looked at himself, he had the weird feeling that his face was a collection of flowing ripples.

He filled the basin and washed, discontent growing in him. He had been on jobs like this for twenty years, most of the time bucking Walt Paddon. More often than not he had lost to Paddon, and the fact added to the sourness that was in him. What had happened today did not sweeten his disposition.

Paddon had foxed him again by staying under cover and using Vicky Starr and Clay Bond in a way that only he could do. Kyle's mistake was in not finding out that Paddon was on the ground, but it was a natural mistake. He hadn't even looked around, for he had known that George Akin was in the country, and he had not expected both of them to be here. It was the first time it had ever happened.

Kyle dried himself and emptied the basin into the slop jar. There was one nice thing about this assignment. It would be his last. If he stopped the Oregon Southern he'd have a job waiting for him back East, a desk job among the big boys in the company who cocked their feet up in front of them and smoked fifty-cent cigars while someone else did the dirty work.

It had always irritated him that he was the one who took the risks while the big guns filled a plush chair with the seat of their pants. Now someone else would be taking the risks. He'd have his plush chair, and he'd have his name in gold letters on the door of his office. Well, he'd earned it, and then some.

They came in, Bronc Main and Cash Taber, Lew Dagget staggering behind them, his yellow eyes a little glazed, his face so battered that the strawberry blotch on his cheek was hardly noticeable.

"Howdy," Kyle said. "Sit down."

Flipping back the cover of the cigar box on his bureau, he picked it up and held it out to his visitors. Main took a cigar, Taber shook his head and rolled a cigarette, and Dagget dropped down on the bed, apparently unaware that the box had been offered to him.

"The meeting kind o' backfired, didn't it, Kyle?" Main

asked maliciously.

Kyle lighted a fresh cigar, masking his face against the anger that Main's words aroused in him. He motioned toward Dagget. "Your rabbit-brained friend yonder didn't help any. You ought to tell him that he can't tackle a woman like he does a man."

Dagget tried to focus his eyes on Kyle. He said, thick-lipped, "She ain't a woman. She's a damned hellcat, and I'll trim her down—"

"Shut up, Lew," Main said curtly. "All right, Kyle. Dagget wasn't smart, but it strikes me you wasn't, neither. Paddon tied you up like a calf ready for branding. Now what the hell are you gonna do about it?"

"Paddon isn't the key to this thing," Kyle said. "Neither is the girl. Clay Bond is, and Clay Bond is the man we've got to work on. The way I see it, we're in luck that he got here just now."

Main snorted. "Luck, is it? Well, mister, I could do without that kind of luck. If I ever get him out on the desert, and the girl, too, I'll—"

"I know," Kyle said impatiently. "He'll disappear like George Akin did. But you're not oversupplied with brains, either, my arrogant friend. You're thinking the sheriff is afraid to tackle you, but you're wrong. You let him get his teeth into something, and you're finished."

"You worry me," Main jeered.

"You'd better worry, and you'd better stop some of your picayunish tricks like sniping at Triangle S cattle. Mule-hide Cotter is no fool. You think you have to bull right into a job, but if you live long enough you'll learn that the long way around is the best way."

Shrugging, Main moved to the window, the cigar tilted upward between his strong teeth. "Wish I was a railroad man. This is a damned sight better cigar than I can afford to buy."

"Won't be long till you'll be smoking better cigars than that," Taber said in a patronizing tone. "Keep the settlers off the desert, and in a year or two you'll have so many cows you'll make the Harney County ranches look like ten-cow spreads."

Main swelled with pride. "That's where I'm headed, son. King of the Desert. That's me, Kyle. Sid Starr might have given me some trouble if he'd lived, but now there's nobody who can stop me. Hear that, Kyle? Nobody. Before I'm done, I'll move down the river and I'll have Triangle S range."

"If the Oregon Southern lays steel across the desert," Kyle said tartly, "you can stop thinking about moving in on Triangle S. You'll be finished on the desert, and you know it."

"Suppose the Columbia & Cascade lays steel across the desert," Taber murmured.

"Yeah, I've thought about that," Main said ominously. "I ain't having no railroad on the desert. I'm telling you, Kyle. If you double-cross me, I'll gut-shoot you the same as I'll gut-shoot George Akin when he signs that letter I writ for him. Savvy?"

"Oh, hell!" Kyle groaned. "I've told you ten times and I'll tell you once more. We're satisfied the way things are. If we build up the Deschutes or across the desert, it will be because we're forced to meet competition."

Dagget lay back on the bed, the springs squeaking. "Wasting time, Bronc. Let'sh go get Bond."

Main fingered the ash from his cigar. "I've got my reasons for stopping Bond's clock, Kyle. I ain't sure I'll take any more orders from you; but I'll listen if you've got anything to say."

Kyle was silent for a moment as doubts rose to plague him. Circumstances had often forced him to throw in with questionable allies, but he had never teamed up with a man he instinctively disliked as he did Bronc Main. Egotistical, proud, lacking a hampering conscience, Main was capable of making the kind of mistake that would force the law to move against him and destroy him.

"You'll take my orders, Bronc," Kyle said tonelessly, "because you know that I can throw too much weight against you if you don't play with me. I'll say another thing that I've said ten times. The one weapon we don't use is murder."

Main winked at Taber. "No murder, he says. What do you want me to do with George Akin, keep him for a pet?"

"You were a damned fool for grabbing him," Kyle snapped. "I don't know what you're going to do with him; but, whatever you do, keep him alive."

Dagget stirred on the bed. "Wasting time, Bronc. I shay we've got to go get Bond."

"All right, Lew," Main said impatiently. "Why'n hell did you send for me, Kyle? If you think your damned sermons about what I can and can't do will—"

"No sermons," Kyle said. "Your boys in town?"

Main nodded. "Sure."

"Bond and Paddon rode out of town together. Where do you figure they're headed?"

"Bond's place on the river that the Starr girl fixed up nice and pretty. Where else?"

"That's my guess," Kyle said. "Now I'm not sure Bond's the kind who'll scare, but it strikes me that it's worth a try. He'll be tickled when he sees what he's got, and he won't want it to go up in smoke. So a little powder burning might be in order. Nothing serious. Just a gesture to make him see which way the wind blows."

"Funny thing," Main said. "I had the same idea, only I ain't sure it'll be just a gesture."

"It had better be," Kyle said sharply. "No killings. Get that straight, now. Bond can't sign a right-of-way agreement if he's dead."

"Sure, sure." Main jerked his head at the door. "We ain't doing no good here. Come on."

They tramped out, Dagget staggering behind Main and Taber. Kyle closed the door and moved to the window, the doubts growing in him. He had a bear by the tail; he couldn't let go, and he couldn't run with the bear.

He stood there for a long time, looking down into the street, mentally cursing the day he had approached Bronc Main. Then he saw the Flying M crew ride by, and the certainty that he had made the biggest mistake of his life filled him with a haunting sense of impending failure. Neither Main nor Taber was with the Flying M hands. Dagget was in the lead, swaying in the saddle.

For a long moment Kyle could not breathe. He knew what this meant. Dagget, half drunk and filled with a bitter hatred for Clay Bond, would lead the attack, and if he had his way he would leave nothing but death and ashes behind him.

Chapter Eight: THE BOND PLACE

CLAY BOND AND WALT PADDON rode directly north from Lava City. The road, little more than two wheel ruts through the junipers, angled away from the Deschutes, took a twisting course down the south wall of Crooked River canyon, and climbed to the north rim. Here where sage and rabbit brush covered the rolling plateau, and there was only an occasional juniper, the irregular sky line of the Cascades came again into view.

There was little talk, for each was deep in his own thoughts. Clay had no definite plan. He had hoped to rebuild on what had been his father's river ranch, knowing that if he did he would have to take up the fight against Sid Starr. If Starr had been alive it would have been as futile as the fight Jim Bond had waged; but he was dead, and that made everything different.

Now, as the sun moved west toward the mountains, the hope that had been shadowed by the certainty of failure rose out of the shadow and began taking form. Vicky was responsible for that. She was her father's daughter, gifted with his drive and certainty of purpose, but lacking the arrogance and selfishness which had given direction to everything he had done. She would, Clay thought, be a good neighbor.

"Funny about this country," Paddon said suddenly. "Within a few miles of us are some of the most recent lava flows in the United States. I'm interested because geology is a hobby with me. If you go up Crooked River and look at the eroded hills, you'll get an idea of what the Paleozoic horizons were."

He looked at Clay, smiling a little, but Clay's response was a grunt.

"Along the John Day River," Paddon went on, "you'll find fossils of the Cenozoic mammals: rhinos, Oreodons, and so on."

Clay pinned his eyes on the railroad man, irritated by his talk because he saw no purpose in it. He said, "I aim to raise beef, Paddon. Not any of the critters you're gabbing about."

Paddon laughed. "Sure. I'm talking about something else. One of the great inviolable laws of life is change. At one time there were mid-Miocene mammals such as the three-toed horse and giraffe camel. Then the ice age came. Those mammals disappeared. Why? Because they couldn't adjust themselves to the changes."

"I suppose the point of your sermon is that your railroad will bring on the ice age and I'll be frozen if I don't adjust myself to it by selling you a right of way."

"Not exactly." Paddon's face showed that he saw no

humor in Clay's words. "Social and economic changes as brought about by man come very fast in comparison to geologic changes, and for that reason my comparison may be poorly made; but I am certain of the workings of this law of change, whether in regard to nature or the affairs of man. The railroad is coming, Bond. Not even Bronc Main can stop it. When it does come, whether this year or ten years from now, it means the end of the open range. It means settlement, barbed wire, and irrigation ditches."

"I know what a railroad does," Clay said testily.

"What are you planning to do with your ranch?"

"Raise beef, I told you. Vicky promised to let me through to the open range. That was where the trouble came between Dad and Sid Starr."

"In your father's day the open range was the only answer," Paddon said earnestly; "but it isn't now. Vicky will let you through, but what about the farmers who will be all over the country?"

Clay held silence a moment, thinking about this. Despite all the railroad news he had heard, he had not changed his thinking to take into account the difference that actual settlement would make. "All right, Paddon. Maybe you can tell me what to do so I won't disappear like them critters you were talking about."

"I can," Paddon said. "In the days of the open range the emphasis was on quantity, not quality. From now on the smart rancher in this country will reverse it. He'll feed, and he'll ship. He'll have a few hundred acres instead of thousands, but he'll make more money than your dad or Sid Starr ever did because he'll be able to ship fat stuff to Portland instead of walking his beef to the Columbia."

They had reached Buck Creek and turned toward the great rift in the plateau that was the canyon of the Deschutes. Triangle S buildings showed to their right, made hazy by the flow of evening shadows across the flat. Strangely enough, Clay did not feel the bitterness he had expected. For the first time in fifteen years, he could think of the Starr ranch without rancor.

He considered the violence of his feelings when he had found out who Vicky was, and again when he had talked to her that morning before reaching Lava City. He saw himself in another light than he had before. He had childishly harbored resentment against a person who was not responsible for the disaster that had wiped out his father.

Vicky had said, "I want to be a neighbor. Don't let your hate for the name Starr make you blind." He could ask no more than that, nor could he doubt the girl's sincerity. Paddon was right. Emphasize quality. Put the fat on and ship by rail. His quarter section would do. He could sell the right of way across his place to Paddon for enough to replace his buildings and restock the ranch.

They reached the rim of the canyon and started down. It was a familiar scene. Clay had looked at it every day from the time he could sit a saddle until he had ridden out of the country. That had been fifteen years ago, but he remembered it as if he had left only yesterday.

They followed the curling trail down the tawny slope, Clay's eyes searching for landmarks. The river made a bend here, and the Bond place lay in that bend on a bench above the stream, one hundred and sixty acres of as good land as a man could find along the Deschutes. Buck Creek came in from the east, bisecting the ranch so that a small dam and a primitive ditch system was all it took to put water on every acre.

Jim Bond had been short of money from the day he had homesteaded here. Much of the time he had let the place go, leaving Clay and Hungry Hale, who was too crippled up to hold down a riding job, to look out for the few cows he owned. He had worked in Prineville or ridden for some outfit up Crooked River and always brought back enough in the fall to buy supplies for the winter. Then he would fret, cursing Sid Starr because the bank in Prineville refused to loan him money to buy a big herd as long as Triangle S blocked him off from the open range to the east.

Now Clay told himself he could expect to find nothing. Fifteen years was a long time to leave a place. The fruit trees would be dead for lack of water, the garden and alfalfa fields grown up in weeds. The corrals and barn might still be standing. If they were, they could be made to do with some patching. Likely the dam was gone and ditches would need to be cleaned out. There was time, before cold weather came, for him to throw up a log cabin that would give him shelter until he had the money to build another house.

The sun was down, leaving a scarlet stain above the western rim as a reminder of its going. Shadows lay in steadily darkening twilight, giving the bench a strange aura of unreality as if it belonged in a different world that was neither night nor day. Clay, close enough now to make out what lay before him, felt first shock and then growing anger.

The rich fragrance of alfalfa was all around. Haystacks loomed high on both sides of the road, and he could hear the liquid whisper of water in the ditches. The fruit trees were a dark patch to his left, the barn and corrals were exactly where he remembered them, and a house stood in the same spot where the original Bond house had stood. The door was open, and lamplight made a yellow patch in the dusk, the center darkened with the long shadow of the old man who stood in the doorway.

Clay swore bitterly. "Paddon, you knew about this?" he challenged.

"Why," Paddon answered softly, "I knew the place was being looked after."

"Looked after," Clay snorted. "Some damned thieving coyote thinks he's jumped it."

He cracked steel to his horse, sweeping ahead. He heard the railroad man cry, "Take it easy, you fool. Nobody's jumped your place," but he didn't stop.

Pulling up in the fringe of lamplight, he stepped down and drew Colt from leather. The oldster had his back to the light so that his face was shadowed, and it was a moment before Clay, looking back into his boyhood memories, recognized Hungry Hale. In the same instant Hale, staring out, recognized his visitor. He called, "You're Clay, ain't you?"

"That's right." Clay slapped him with his voice. "Who's claiming this place?"

Hale limped toward Clay, his hand extended. "It's good to see you, boy. Fifteen years make a man out of a kid. I wouldn't have knowed you if I hadn't figgered you was about due. Welcome home, Clay."

"My home was a pile of ashes when I left here," Clay said curtly, ignoring the hand. "What's going on?"

Hale's hand dropped, and his voice showed his hurt. "This is your place, Clay. Nobody's claiming it from you. Every year I took the money you sent me and paid your taxes. Right now it's the most valuable place on the river 'cause a railroad—"

"I know," Clay said impatiently. "I figgered that was why you sent for me; but you ain't told who built this house and fixed the ditches and cut the hay. Who did it?"

"Vicky," Hale said heavily. "She's a mighty fine girl, Vicky is. She couldn't undo all the coyote tricks old Sid did, but she's sure tried."

"Vicky."

Something went out of Clay Bond then. He had believed in Vicky Starr, sensing a genuineness about her he had never felt in another woman. Now that faith was swept away by what Hale said. No one, not even Vicky Starr, would build a house on land that was not hers unless she saw a chance to make her money back.

"Come in," Hale said. "I ain't got supper on, not knowing when you'd be here, but I've got some sowbelly and cackleberries in the pantry. I'll get a fire going right away."

"Who gets the hay?" Clay demanded roughly.

"Vicky's been using it, but she says she'll pay you whatever is fair for rent."

"You're damned right she will," Clay flung at the old man. "She don't need to get the notion that putting up a house is gonna square using my place. I suppose she figgered she'd get it rent-free, and I suppose old Sid used it all the time he was alive. He didn't have to get title. He just shot Dad and moved in. That right, Hungry?"

Paddon had pulled up. He said, "You're being more of a damned fool than I gave you credit for, Bond."

Clay moved around his horse. "Sure, that'd be the way you'd figger. Vicky and you are on the same side of the fence. She gives you a right of way for a dollar, and you back her up for stealing my place. You'd better keep out of it, Paddon." He wheeled back to Hale. "You ain't answered me about Starr."

"You called it right," the old man said. "Sid never done nothing good in his life except sire Vicky. She's been running Triangle S since he died, and she's the one that fixed up your barn and the corrals; and she built this house. She said you'd be back some day, and she wanted it to be in shape so you could start making a living off your place right away."

"She never knew me. She was just a kid when I left. How'd she know I was coming back?"

"I told her," Hale said. "She's the best friend I've got. I had a hell of a time after Sid beefed your dad. Swamped out in a Prineville saloon. Couldn't get nothing better to do. I just wasn't no good no more. Then, after Sid died, Vicky took me in." He sucked in a long breath. "Now make up your mind, Clay. If you're aiming to start fighting Vicky like Jim fought Sid, I'm riding out of here tonight."

"He isn't that much of a fool," Paddon broke in. "Look, Bond. You're all mixed up. Maybe your pride's got in front of you. Or maybe you hate the name Starr so much you can't think straight, but—"

"Stay out of it, Paddon," Clay said ominously.

"In Lava City you asked me how I got Vicky on my side," the railroad man went on. "Now I'll tell you in one-syllable words so you can understand. She's on my side because she knows the Oregon Southern will build a railroad, and the railroad's an obsession with her; but if you're going to be greedy you'll throw a monkey wrench into things good. She's done a lot for you, so—"

"So I repay the favor by selling you a right of way for a dollar. Not me, friend. You can all go to hell. I never saw anybody who didn't figger on filling their own pockets first and taking care of the other gent later. If Vicky sold you a right of way for a dollar, she's got other ideas how to make it up. Maybe I'd better get an idea, too. Like talking to Hugh Kyle again."

Clay stepped back into the saddle and rode on to the barn. Paddon said, "Get supper started, Hale," and followed.

Clay had lighted a lantern and was throwing hay into the manger when Paddon came in and stripped gear from his mount. Clay said, a deep fury working in him, "To let you and Hungry tell it, Vicky must be an angel. Maybe you're on the level thinking she is, but I ain't swallowing the notion. Not about Sid Starr's girl. She had some kind of an idea for peeling the bark off my back, or she'd never have built that house."

Paddon waited until Clay came through a vacant stall to stand beside him. Then he said, "She's about as near to being an angel as anybody I ever saw. Take this business of going into the desert after George Akin. She's got an idea Main's holding him prisoner. Now a real selfish person would let it go, but not Vicky. She won't send Mulehide Cotter—he's her foreman—because she says a man would get killed, so she tried doing the job herself."

Clay snorted. "After what happened at Benton's, I guess she knows what Main will do to her when he thinks he's in his own territory."

He left the barn and walked on through the darkness to the river, listening to its steady growl as it rolled northward to the Columbia, gnawing a still deeper gut in its slow merciless way as it had been doing through eons of time. Night had fallen quickly, as he remembered it in the canyon bottom. Across the river a sheer rock wall rose directly from the water's edge. There was no room along the cliff for twin rails. Geography had dropped a fortune into his lap, and only a fool would not reach for that fortune.

He built a smoke and fired it, the match flame throwing a brief light across his dark, lean-jawed face. As he moved toward the small ridge north of the house he saw Paddon cross the light patch in front of the door and go in.

A vague uneasiness gripped him. He wanted to believe in Vicky, and the desire warred with logic. Anyone else he had known would have had some swindle in mind before going to the expense she had here. If on the other hand she was on the level, he did owe her something, and she would want him to sign with Paddon tonight. She had said that when he had been back for a while he would believe in the things she did and would fight for them. To hell with that! He'd paid taxes on this place for fifteen years. The Starrs had used it, and he couldn't do anything about that; but he could do one thing. He could make Paddon pay and pay right.

He was still thinking about Paddon when he came to his mother's grave. There was a tight wire fence around it that had not been there when he had gone away. He found a gate, opened it, and went in. Striking a match, he held the flame close to an upright board. The name *Jim Bond* was cut upon it. He straightened, the match flame running along the stick until it burned him. He dropped it, puzzling over this. Hale had written that his father was buried in Prineville.

Another match showed Clay a second board beside the one he had just seen. Carved in the crooked letters a child would make were the words, *Martha Bond.* Weather had worn them until they were almost unintelligible, but they were the same crude letters he had cut on the headboard three days after his mother had died.

Straightening, he dropped the match and wiped a hand across his face. He was remembering things long forgotten, the doleful preacher from Prineville; the hollow echo of clods on the pine coffin; his father saying, "I should never have brought her here. The country was too hard for her."

Slowly Clay moved back through the fence and closed the gate. He stood there a long moment, staring at the high canyon wall, a black barrier against the sky. He asked himself why his mother had died, why his father had said the country was too hard for her. Then, for the first time, he began to understand Vicky Starr and what she believed in. He knew the answers to his questions, and he made himself admit it.

His mother had died when she was thirty, younger than Clay was now. Everywhere in the West where pioneers had settled, the story was the same. People dying when they were still young, cheated out of most of their years because life was too hard, because they had to do without the things that could have taken some of the labor out of their lives. Those were the things they could not afford because the distance from the railroad made transportation cost more than their original price.

Clay turned back to the house, fists clenched at his sides. In fifteen years the situation had not changed. The wives of settlers who were moving onto irrigated land below Lava City would face the same life his mother had faced, and many of them would die before they were thirty for the same reason his mother had died.

The railroad was the answer to a lot of things. Vicky understood that, and her understanding had made her try to do something about it. Then his thoughts turned inward. Some day he would be married, and he might stand beside his wife's grave the way his father had once stood beside Martha Bond's grave, and his conscience would put him in hell. Within the hour Walt Paddon had said, "If you're going to be greedy you'll throw a monkey wrench into things good."

Clay stepped into the house, where coffee fragrance spiced the air. Hungry Hale was frying eggs, a bent, dirty-headed old man who was little more than Vicky Starr's pensioner. He stood with his weight on his one good leg, the short one barely touching the floor. Clay remembered the day a mean horse had slammed into him and pinned him against a corral post. His leg had never healed right. If anybody owed Hungry Hale a pension it was Clay Bond, not Vicky Starr.

"I thought you wrote Dad was buried in Prineville," Clay said.

Hale looked up from the frying-pan. "He was; but after Vicky started running Triangle S she allowed Jim oughta be buried beside your ma, so we moved the body."

Paddon said, his voice razor-sharp, "A man who sees things like you do, Bond, would figure she was going to make him pay for it."

Clay wheeled on him with anger. Then it was gone. The words were justified. "All right," he said heavily. "I won't throw a monkey wrench into your railroad building. But I don't figger on signing a right-of-way agreement for a dollar, neither."

"I don't expect you to. What do you think the right of way is worth?"

"I ain't saying yet." Clay turned to Hale. "Hungry, I didn't shake your hand. I've got no apologies to make except that I didn't savvy. I ain't real sure I do yet, but I am sure of one thing—I'm beholden to you for keeping my taxes paid."

He held out his hand, knowing he could not blame the old man for ignoring it. But Hale took it quickly.

"It's all right, Clay. I'm glad you're home, mighty glad."

Chapter Nine: RACE WITH TIME

IN ONE REGARD it was a fault for a person to hold to an idea with the tenacity of purpose and fervency of spirit which bound Vicky to her belief that the Oregon Southern must be supported without question and without qualification —a fault because it colored every thought and feeling that she had. It made her worry over George Akin's safety; it made her trust Walt Paddon completely. At the same time it made her hate and fear Bronc Main and Hugh Kyle. As for Clay Bond, her feeling would be influenced by the decision he made about the railroads.

Sid Starr had been proud of Vicky's beauty, even as a child. To him she was a toy to be dressed in the most expensive clothes he could buy in Prineville, to be trotted on his knee and played with when he had time, and to be protected from the rough and primitive surroundings in which they lived.

As she grew older his notion of protection had meant a clash of wills. He could no more keep Vicky within the walls of the Triangle S ranch house than he could have made a house cat out of a mountain lion, for she had a wild and turbulent spirit that could not be bound. If he had lived that clash would eventually have led to open rebellion; but he had died, and his death had freed her.

In the years that followed, Vicky reversed almost everything Sid Starr had done; but there was one small thing she did not change, a matter which had never actually entered her consciousness. Her father had not taken her to Prineville often; but every time he had, it had been the accepted thing for them to go together to Old Peter Delong's dry-goods store and buy cloth for a new dress. After his death she had continued the practice, the one extravagance which she allowed herself.

When she left Clay Bond on Main Street, she went at once to Old Peter Delong's new store. Old Peter still owned the store in Prineville; but within the last month he had opened a second store in Lava City and was running it himself, confident that within a few years the new town would become the metropolis of central Oregon.

He stepped out of the back room when he heard Vicky come in. He called, "I was afraid you'd leave town without coming in, Miss Starr. I just received a new shipment of dress goods from Triumph."

He had always called her Miss Starr, even when her father had lifted her as a child to the counter, saying in his loud voice, "Take your pick, girl. The best in the house is none too good for Sid Starr's daughter."

Vicky laughed. "Old Peter, did you ever see me leave town without buying a new dress?"

He scratched his nose. He had been known as Old Peter

from the first day he had come to central Oregon. No one actually knew his age, although it was commonly said he was over a hundred but looked like a young man of eighty. He had long ago lost the last hair on his head; his parchmentlike skin seemed too scant to cover the bones of his face adequately, but his dark eyes were as bright as a schoolboy's.

Now his eyes twinkled as he said, "No, I have never seen you leave town without a new dress, but I have never seen so much excitement on the street, either."

She laughed again, not because of what she said but because she felt good. Clay Bond had set Hugh Kyle back on his heels, and Kyle had stomped away, as angry a man as she had ever seen. More than that, Clay had ridden away with Paddon. It was enough to fill her with the pleasant warmth which rose from the knowledge that a victory had been won. She did not doubt that Clay had been convinced she was right, that she had tempered his natural bitterness for her and her name, and that they could be neighbors.

"Did you see the fight?" she asked.

"That I did. I have no love for violence, but this one time I enjoyed watching a fight. Dagget has had a licking coming for a long time." He shook his head, dark eyes somber. "A bully when he's sober and a monster when he's drunk. And young Bond! A man, Miss Starr, a man if I ever saw one."

She nodded agreement. "He's all of that."

"I knew his father well," Old Peter went on, "although I remember Clay only as a snub-nosed kid. I never would have known him, looking at him now. But it isn't just his looks. It's the feeling you get looking at him. Jim Bond gave you that same feeling. I recollect the day he met your father in Prineville—"

"Let me see the new dress goods," Vicky cut in, turning

toward the counter.

"Of course, of course," he said, sensing that he had made a mistake. He stepped behind the counter, motioning with a clawlike hand toward the bolts of cloth on the shelves. "Taffeta. Poplin. Bombazine. A fine assortment, Miss Starr. Now you go ahead and look. Take your time. I have some work to do in the back room."

He fled, leaving Vicky alone. For a long time she stood motionless, staring at the shelves, the good feeling gone. She had forgotten for the moment that her father had killed Jim Bond. She had wanted to forget it; she had hoped Clay could forget it. Now she knew the hope was a foolish one. She thought again, as she had thought so many times, that, of all the people who had suffered at Sid Starr's hand, Clay Bond had suffered the most.

It was expecting too much to think that he could understand how she had tried to undo what her father had done, how much she wanted a railroad to help the country because Sid Starr had held it back with his greedy, roughshod tactics. Clay would not even understand why she had built the new house for him, confident that some day he would return. It would take both time and patience on her part to dissolve his bitterness.

Then a new worry rose in her. He might hate her so much he would bargain with Hugh Kyle simply because she favored the Oregon Southern. The way he had dealt with Kyle a few minutes before might prove nothing except that he was working for the best price he could get. She could not blame him; she could not blame him for anything he might do.

She lost all sense of time. She took one bolt after another off the shelves, felt of the cloth and studied the pattern; but the pleasure that usually came from picking a dress would not come today. Suddenly loud talk from the street beat against her consciousness, she heard horses, and she ran to the front door, calling, "Old Peter."

He hurried out of the back room, answering the urgency in her voice, and reached the door in time to see the Flying M crew leave town with Lew Dagget in front.

"Dagget's drunk," Vicky breathed. "What does it mean?"

"Bronc Main owns a big piece of range north of here," Old Peter said. "Maybe he's sending his crew out there."

"You know better," she said impatiently. "There isn't a Flying M steer within ten miles of the Deschutes."

He scratched his nose, staring after the riders. "There's trouble wherever Main goes, but he isn't with his boys."

"You're thinking the same thing I am," Vicky whispered. "Clay left with Paddon awhile ago. They'll go to the Bond place. Main will guess that, too. If they were dead—" She stopped, biting her lip.

The store man said, "If they were dead, the Oregon Southern would have a hard time getting a right of way across the Bond place. That's what you were going to say, isn't it, Miss Starr?"

"But they won't be dead. I'll see to that."

She ran toward Royden's livery stable. Old Peter called, "Your dress—"

"I won't buy one today," she cried, and ran on.

When she rode out of town a few minutes later, heading north, the dust kicked up by the Flying M men still hung in the air like a gray haze. They would not hurry, she thought; it was unlikely they would attack before dark. Clay Bond had shown the night before at Benton's roadhouse and again today in Lava City that he was not a man to be taken lightly. Dagget would know that Hungry Hale was at the Bond place. Walt Paddon would be there, too. That made three men, enough to put up a hard fight.

A mile north of Lava City she glimpsed the Flying M hands ahead of her and left the road, making a wide swing eastward through the junipers. They were scattered here, and she made good time for an hour. Then she was forced to ride more cautiously, for she was in open country covered by sage and rabbit brush with numerous lava outcroppings that made ragged, steep-walled barriers. She circled them, wasting time, or rode carefully across them.

One thing was in her favor. Dagget and his men would not expect this from her. Perhaps it would have been wiser to keep to the road and pass them, for they would have naturally assumed that she was merely riding home. She angled back to the road, hoping to reach the Crooked River crossing ahead of them.

They were not in sight when she reached the south rim of Crooked River canyon. The sun was low over the Cascades now, throwing out brilliant scarlet banners above the snow peaks. Dusk was not far away. She dropped down the narrow road, riding recklessly, reached the bottom, and thundered across the bridge. The steep north wall slowed her. She pulled up at the top to blow her horse and, looking back, saw them start down the other side.

The awful fear that she would be too late gripped her spine and brought a sick emptiness into her middle. She did not know if she would find her crew at the ranch; she did not even know whether Mulehide Cotter had gone back to Triangle S after the meeting in Lava City, or what he would say when she told him that Clay Bond needed help. She went on, twilight deepening until it was a vast purple blanket flung out over this land, and she knew that if she lived to be a hundred years old she would never make a more important ride than this.

Chapter Ten: ATTACK

THE HOUSE THAT VICKY STARR HAD BUILT for Clay was not a large one. It had a living-room, a kitchen, and one bedroom, with little furniture; but it was a house, and it would do for a womanless ranch. Clay finished supper, rolled a smoke, and, taking a lamp, looked around. There were no carpets or rugs on the rough board floors; but the ceilings and walls were papered, and the house was clean. Hungry Hale had seen to that.

It had certainly cost Vicky both money and trouble. Clay returned to the kitchen and set the lamp on the table, not meeting Hale's or Paddon's eyes. Old suspicions were hard to kill. If he had never come back, Triangle S would have gone on using this place, and Vicky would have needed a house for Hungry Hale or anyone else who stayed here.

"What do you think of it?" Hale asked.

"It'll do."

Clay moved across the front room and stood in the open doorway, gaze working across the bench to the river, which glittered in the starlight like a curling flow of black obsidian. Above it the cliff rose two hundred feet before it slanted back, a bleak barrier without life. It brought his mind again to the railroad. Everything, it seemed, reminded him of the twin lines of steel that would soon be pushing south from the Columbia. Just how soon they came depended upon him, or so Walt Paddon and Vicky Starr would say.

A man returning to his childhood home should not expect to find things as he remembered them; yet Clay had clung to the impressions he had received as a boy. He had thought that nowhere else in the world were sage smells so spicy or the alfalfa as fragrant as here along the Deschutes, nowhere else was there a river so clear and wild and cold.

It had been an adolescent world when he had left, a world filled with violence and fear and hate, all centering around Sid Starr. Now it was an adult world, and he realized, standing in the doorway, that the sage was not so spicy as he had remembered, the alfalfa not so fragrant, the Deschutes not so swift and boisterous. Even the great west wall was far from the gigantic thing he had been picturing.

Clay built a smoke, lighted it, and stared into the darkness. It was entirely still except for the rattle of dishes from the kitchen. Then that died. The cigarette went cold in his mouth. The emptiness was in him that comes to a man when adult realities fall below his boyhood memories. There was this moment when life stood still and he floundered through a fifteen-year vacuum. In the kitchen Walt Paddon and Hungry Hale were silent.

Clay was not sure when the warning beat into his consciousness. He had been vaguely aware of horse sounds from the trail winding down the east side of the canyon before the prickle along his spine jarred him into cognizance of it. He threw the cold cigarette into the yard, keening the still night air for the faint click of steel on rock, a whispered order, the whicker of a horse.

"Hungry!" he said softly.

Both men came to him, Hale asking, "What's up?"

Clay stepped through the door into the yard. "Listen."

A moment of silence, and then Walt Paddon took a long breath. "Bronc Main is persistent, Bond. We're in trouble."

"Why?"

"The sides were drawn in Lava City today," Paddon answered. "It's you and me and Vicky against Main and Dagget and Hugh Kyle. It's the Oregon Southern against the Columbia & Cascade."

"I don't savvy. Don't seem to me—"

"The Columbia & Cascade is playing a blocking game," Paddon said impatiently. "They'll build only when and if we force them to. If you're dead and we don't have a signed agreement giving us a right of way across your land, we'll have a hell of a time. Kyle can go into court and tie the Oregon Southern up till hell freezes."

"There's a dozen of 'em," Hale said worriedly. "They ain't up to no good, or they wouldn't be so damned quiet."

"Come on," Clay said, and swung into the house.

He moved the lamp from the kitchen into the front room and set it on the desk so that shafts of yellow light fell into the front yard from the windows and door. He asked, "Got a gun, Hungry?"

"A Winchester in the bedroom."

"Get it and all the shells you've got. What about you, Paddon?"

"I've got a thirty-two in my pocket."

Clay snorted. "Popgun. Why in hell don't you pack a man's gun?"

"To tell the truth, I didn't think we'd be in this fix. I expected Kyle to tie us up with some legal tricks, but I didn't look for murder. That'll be Main, Bond. He isn't one to forget you backed him down, and Dagget won't forget you licked him."

"Come on," Clay said, and went into the kitchen and out through the back door.

"What are you aiming to do?" Hale asked.

"Come on," Clay repeated irritably.

They followed him through the darkness to the barn, Hale growling disapproval.

Clay swung the barn door open and asked, "Got any grain, Hungry?"

"There's five, six sacks of oats over in the corner."

"Give me a hand, Paddon," Clay ordered.

"I don't take to the notion of letting 'em fire the house," Hale said bitterly. "What's the matter with you, Clay? Your pap was always one to fight."

"We'll fight." Clay dropped a sack of oats in the doorway and went back for another. "If we stayed in the house they'd slaughter us. Watch what they do and you'll see I'm right."

They piled the six sacks of oats in the doorway. Crouching behind them, Clay drew his gun. He asked, "This is the only door, isn't it, Hungry?"

"Yeah," Hale grunted. "Just like it used to be."

"Keep quiet. They'll walk into that patch of light. When they do, give it to 'em. Ever kill a man, Paddon?"

"No," the railroad man breathed.

"You'd better, tonight," Clay said. "Cash Taber is the one to watch. He's smart. That's why he's Main's ramrod."

They waited, crouched behind the oat sacks, guns in their hands. They could see the front of the house. The lamp shining through the open door and windows gave the only spots of light in a black world. The horsemen were close now, in the alfalfa probably not more than fifty feet from the house.

"What are they waiting on?" Paddon whispered.

"Looking things over," Clay answered. "If we had been in sight we'd be full of lead by now. That's why they're sneaking up so damned careful, hoping they'll get a bead on one of us."

Another long moment, each second dragging. Paddon was breathing in long hard pants, Hale sucking in short breaths that whistled as they left his lungs. Clay smiled faintly at the tension he felt in them. To him this was an old and too-familiar situation that he could face calmly.

There was the sound of horses, then, and presently Lew Dagget's great voice boomed into the silence. "Bond! Are you inside?"

They waited, the stillness mocking him. Clay whispered, "Taber must not be there. Dagget ain't so smart. He'll move in. Get ready."

He had called it right. The sound of horses was close now. One of the men cursed, and Dagget shouted, "Bond!

We want to talk to you."

Clay could make out the vague shapes of horses and riders. They formed a wide arc before the house, and another moment of silence dragged by before Dagget said, "You don't need to play hard to get, Bond, damn you. I'm giving you ten seconds. Then we're coming in."

Saddle leather squeaked as men dismounted; the metallic click of guns being brought to cock rode the air. There was a rush for the door. For an instant a dozen men were massed in the patch of light in front of the house, Lew Dagget in the lead. That instant Clay began shooting, Paddon and Hale firing before the echo of his first shot had died.

The shots brought pandemonium to Dagget's party. Two men went down. Others yelled in agony. There was a wild scurrying for the cover of darkness. Horses bucked away from the house. Men grabbed at reins. Some swung into saddles; others missed and sprawled in the dirt, making the night hideous with their cursing. All the time Clay was shooting. He emptied his Colt, grabbed the Winchester out of Hale's hands, pulled trigger, levered another shell into the chamber, and fired again, laying his bullets into the scattering mass of men and horses.

"He's in the barn!" Dagget bawled. "A hundred dollars to the man that gets him!"

But there was no rush for the barn. Clay called, "You don't seem to have any takers, Dagget. Why don't you earn the money yourself?"

Suddenly there was quiet as Dagget's men recovered from their panic. Clay gave the rifle back to Hale, saying, "Load it." He punched the empties out of his .45 and thumbed new shells into the cylinder. "Load up, Paddon. They may try a rush, though I doubt if they've got the guts."

"Sorry," Paddon said apologetically. "I don't have any

more shells."

"I've only got this one box," Hale said. "I never figgered on this. Don't have much need for shooting. Just a deer now and then."

Exuberance faded from Clay. He swore softly, only then realizing the precariousness of their position. If Dagget's men sat down for a siege!

"Looks like we'd better go easy on the shells," he said.

There was silence, broken occasionally by a shot from one of Dagget's men. The two who had fallen in front of the house were still there, bodies curled in the grotesque fashion of men who had died the instant they had fallen.

"I'm not sure this is smart," Paddon said. "What do you aim to do, Bond?"

"I aim to sit it out. You and Hungry can saddle up and ride. Let 'em know who you are. It's me Dagget wants."

"I'm not that kind," Paddon said with some anger.

"Wouldn't do no good if you was," Hale added. "That bunch don't want nobody getting away who could identify 'em."

Clay held his silence, thinking. There were still nine or ten of them, scattered around the front of the barn. They were firing with considerable regularity, bullets ripping through the flimsy barn wall or snapping overhead through the doorway. Occasionally one would go *thwack* into an oat sack, and Paddon would instinctively flatten himself into the barn litter.

"Railroad building in the far West," Clay murmured. "How do you like it, Paddon?"

"I don't like it," Paddon muttered. "Looks to me like we're trapped. There's so much lead flying around we'd get tagged the instant we walked through the door."

"They ain't pushing us," Clay said.

He made a small opening between the top oat sacks and poked his rifle barrel through it. He waited until one of

Dagget's men fired, and shot instantly at the flash. A man cried out, and he knew he had made a hit. The firing stopped. He laughed softly.

"Maybe we're trapped, Paddon, but Dagget don't know how to get his badgers out of the hole. I guess it'd be safe for you and Hungry to make a run for it."

"I told you I wasn't that kind." Fear honed a fine edge to Paddon's voice. "I'll see it through."

"Triangle S is the nearest help," Clay said thoughtfully. "Reckon Vicky'd send her boys?"

"Sure she would," Hale answered, "but it's a hell of a long ways on foot, and we couldn't get a horse out of here without drawing bullets like honey draws flies."

That was true. Clay handed him the Winchester. He had hoped that the first flurry of shooting which had taken its toll would discourage Dagget, but apparently it had only stiffened his determination.

"Funny thing, Paddon," he said. "I've been wondering whether it's Kyle's money or Dagget's and Main's hate that's back of this."

"Both, but it wouldn't be Kyle's idea. He's got a conscience, and I doubt that Main has." Paddon was silent a moment, and then added, "We can't sit here waiting to be shot, Bond. If we both get killed tonight it'll be a long time before any steel is laid up the Deschutes."

"I reckon," Clay agreed.

Paddon surprised him. Any way a man looked at it, it wasn't a pleasant thing to lie behind a pile of oat sacks waiting for a bullet to tag him; but Paddon had not folded. He possessed a hard core of courage, and grew in Clay's respect.

"I think I'll try a run for it," he said. "Maybe I can get help. My job is bigger than me, Bond, or any human life. This is just part of the risk a man takes. Same as a powder blast going off in your face, or having a rock bounce off your head from a cliff."

"You don't mean that? Riding out of here?"

"I mean it," Paddon said tonelessly. "If I can get help before sunup, maybe you can hold out."

"Suppose I don't sign your right-of-way agreement?"

"Then you'd better be making up your mind," Paddon answered hotly, "because if that's the way you feel you can lie here and be bullet bait for all I care."

Clay laughed. "I thought that was the way it worked. Nothing comes before the railroad, does it?"

"Damned little," Paddon snapped.

"We ain't being pushed yet. Let's sit it out for a while."

At once Clay knew they couldn't, for some of Dagget's men had worked around to the side of the barn. A bullet ripped through the thin pine boards to slap into a manger across the runway.

Quickly he moved three oat sacks to the side, but now they were only one sack high and gave poor protection. He said, "Keep down on your bellies."

"No use waiting," Paddon muttered. "I'll saddle my horse and get out of here."

"Don't try it," Clay said. "This ain't your kind of game. You'd never get through."

"I can't ride fast no more," Hale said dispiritedly. "Kind of puts it up to you, Clay."

"I was thinking that."

Still Clay didn't move. Hale had been right in saying Dagget would not leave anyone behind to identify them. Clay's departure would not save Paddon's and Hale's lives. Their only weapon would be Hale's Winchester, and neither he nor Paddon could shoot straight enough to hold off a rush.

Paddon could stand the strain no longer. "What are you going to do, Bond?" he demanded frantically.

The firing outside died down and then began again

with renewed fury. Clay snapped a shot at a gun flash to tell Dagget's bunch they were still able to shoot. Then he said, "Anything we do is wrong, Paddon. I can't ride off and leave you two, and we can't stay here. Sooner or later we'll run out of shells, and then it's the windup." He paused, and added thoughtfully, "There's no moon for another hour or two. Maybe we can crawl out and get to the river."

"They'd spread out and find us," Hale objected. "Even if we got to the river, where would we go?"

"They'll keep the trail guarded, but we can go up Buck Creek. The canyon's narrow. Be easy enough to hold 'em off."

"Won't do," Hale said. "You might make it, but it'd take an Injun to belly out of here. Me and Paddon ain't that good Injuns."

That, too, was true; but if Clay went on foot he would be too late to get help from Triangle S. A sense of defeat settled upon him. It was death if they stayed and death if they attempted a run for it.

"I've been in some tights before," he said finally, "but I always had enough ammunition to make the other fellow think twice before he rooted me out."

A burst of firing broke out at the side of the barn. He hugged the ground, wondering if it was the forerunner of a rush and decided not. Dagget and his bunch would have no stomach for an open attack. Then he knew what the shooting meant. Through a crack in the back side of the barn he saw a burst of flame. He emptied his gun in that direction, bullets ripping through the thin boards. Someone yelled, and there was the thud of driving boots as a man fled. The flame flared up, burned brightly for a moment, and died down.

"I wondered when they'd think of burning us out," Clay said sourly. "One of 'em throwed a torch and ran;

but the next time they might toss it close enough to catch the wall."

"I guess we ride," Hale said.

"I reckon," Clay agreed. "If they got a fire going, they could see us good enough to pick us off."

He rose and turned toward the horses. Instantly he dropped back, for at the moment there was no firing and the sound of running horses came to him clearly. A great voice broke across the bench. "There they are, sheriff. Take 'em in."

It was a miracle. Clay could understand it no other way. He called, "It's Dagget," and grabbing up Hale's Winchester, began firing, keeping his bullets low so that none would hit the bunch riding in.

A yell went up from Dagget's party. Their horses had been gathered after that first pile-up in front of the house, and now Dagget's men wasted no time getting into saddles. They swung wide into the alfalfa field and made for the trail up the east side of the canyon. There was some firing from the posse, but none of Dagget's men answered.

Clay stepped out of the barn, letting out a high squall of derision. A moment later the posse thundered into the yard, a man calling, "Everybody all right?"

"We ain't even got a nick," Clay answered, "but there's a couple of polecats laying over there in front of the house."

Hale limped across the yard, asking, "How the hell did you know about this, Mulehide?"

"Vicky guessed what was up." The Triangle S foreman stepped down, laughing in a deep, belly rumble. "Say, didn't they take out of here! Just like rabbits. Long as they had you holed up they was mighty tough; but get somebody coming in from their back side, and they lit out in a hurry."

There were only five men in the posse. They moved

toward the house, Cotter stooping to look at the two dead men. He rose, grunting, "A couple of Bronc Main's toughs, which same ain't a surprise."

Clay's gaze swung around the five of them. None carried a star. "Which one of you is the sheriff?"

Cotter laughed and slapped himself on the chest. "I'm as good as any. I yelled that 'cause I figgered them boys wouldn't want to tangle with the sheriff. Main's been walking purty easy in this end of the county on account of he don't want no lawman nosing around in the desert."

"Hell, you ain't no posse," Clay said. "Good thing Dagget didn't know that, and good thing he didn't know there was only five of you."

Cotter shrugged. "Aw, I don't guess it made much difference. That hombre wasn't looking for an even fight."

"How did Vicky guess what Dagget would do?"

Cotter rolled a smoke, a stocky square-jawed man whose eyes lingered on Clay's face. He sealed the cigarette and slid it into his mouth before he said, "She saw Main's outfit leave town heading north. Wasn't no need of a dozen cowhands heading downstream from Lava City, so she added everything up and got the right answer." He fired his cigarette. "Looks to me like we just got here in time."

"We're mighty glad to see you," Paddon said in a grateful tone. "I was trying to think what would look good on my tombstone."

Cotter guffawed. "That was a right good subject to be thinking on. Well, we might as well ride. They won't be back." He turned to one of his men. "Andy, you and Slim catch up them horses we saw when we came in. We'll take this carrion in for you, Bond, and let the sheriff have a look at 'em."

"I'll be over in the morning to thank Miss Starr," Clay said grudgingly.

He had saved Vicky's life, and now she had saved his in

turn; but he hated the idea of being beholden to a Starr. Suddenly he felt the pressure of Paddon's eyes. He was aware, too, of the silence, of Cotter's wintry face as the man stared at him.

"I never knowed you or your dad," Cotter said finally. "I never even knowed Sid Starr. Not being here on the Deschutes when the ruckus between your dad and Sid came off, I didn't know firsthand what it was all about; but, from what I hear, it wasn't all Sid's fault."

"Why in hell wasn't it?" Clay flung at him. "He had us boxed in, didn't he? He killed Dad, didn't he?"

"From what I hear that's all true," Cotter agreed. "But I say that when a ruckus gets to the shooting stage the wrong ain't all on one side. Sid would have been a fool, letting your dad through to the open range on account of there was only so much and he aimed to use it. Every cow that came on it from some other outfit meant there was less for his. Besides, don't forget he took a hell of a beating from Jim Bond. Then Jim goes gunning for him. Ain't nothing Sid could do but drill him."

It was right, and Clay knew it; but years of hating and years of blaming a man could not be wiped out of his consciousness by any amount of logic. He said coldly, "Starr killed Dad. Nothing changes that, and it gravels me like hell to have to thank Triangle S for saving my hide."

"Now, mebbe it does," Cotter said mildly; "but Vicky ain't nothing like her old man. Ain't nobody that knows her, me or Hungry, there, or Paddon, but what would go out and jump into the river if she asked us to. That's what we think of her. What was done tonight was because Vicky said to. You say you're gonna thank her. All right. There's one way you can do it. Sign that right-of-way agreement for Paddon."

"The damned railroad," Clay exploded. "That's all I've

heard since I got back."

"That's all any of us hears. It's what Vicky lives for. It means the end of Triangle S; but, if that's what Vicky wants, that's what she'll get. You hear, Bond?"

It was a threat, not too well veiled, and the anger in Clay, stirred so many times since he had stopped at Benton's roadhouse, flamed again. He said, "I'm thanking you for saving our hides, Cotter, but that don't make me sit around while you tell me what I've got to do."

"I think mebbe you'd better sign that agreement before you come around Triangle S." Cotter wheeled toward his horse. "Let's ride."

Clay watched them go, the anger dying in him. Paddon and Hale stood behind him, saying nothing, but he knew what they were thinking. He was in a fight, and if he stayed he'd be in it until the road was built or the Oregon Southern was beaten. The least he could do was to sign the right-of-way agreement Paddon wanted. There was no real reason why he shouldn't unless he wanted to play Kyle against Paddon, and he would not do that. Still, a stubbornness was in him. They were forcing him, and Clay Bond was not a man to be pushed. Even by a pretty girl like Vicky Starr.

Clay made a slow turn to face Walt Paddon. The railroad man still wore his cone-peaked hat and corduroy suit that was dirty and smelly with barn litter; he still seemed frail and slender and too weak for this land of hate and violence. Now Clay knew that his appearance was a sort of disguise, that actually, in his own way, he was as strong as Hugh Kyle or Bronc Main or any of the others.

"It strikes me," Clay said, "that your fishing trip was just a stall to come here."

Paddon chewed his lower lip for a moment. Then he said, "That's right. I have secured signed right-of-way agreements for most of our route up the canyon and across the plateau to Lava City. This is the one spot we're stuck. I'm being frank because I take you to be an honest man. Hale said you'd be along, so I waited in Lava City, speaking to every stranger I saw until I met you. So I'm here, you're here, and we need this agreement signed before actual construction starts. How about it?"

"Yeah, I'll sign," Clay breathed, taking a perverse pleasure in holding out. "I offered Kyle the right of way for one hundred thousand."

Paddon's lips tightened. "You're joshing, of course."

"It was a little high," Clay agreed. "I'll make it fifty thousand to you."

Paddon said sourly, "You're still a little high," and turned into the house.

"Your dad would not have been that kind of a hog," Hungry Hale said in disgust, and followed Paddon.

For a long time Clay stood motionless, staring at the great cliff across the river. The moon tipped over the eastern rim, its pale light giving a weird unreality to the river and the canyon bottom.

Tomorrow he would see Vicky Starr. He was not being a hog. He wanted to be fair to himself and to the railroad and to the country, but he wasn't sure what figure would be fair. Tomorrow Vicky Starr would tell him. He felt his natural stubbornness build a wall within him, for already, even before he saw her, he could feel the pressure of her will, this slim, blue-eyed girl who held the unswerving loyalty of men like Mulehide Cotter.

Chapter Eleven: TRIANGLE S

CLAY ATE BREAKFAST with Paddon and Hale, and when he was finished he rose. "I'm riding to Triangle S. A hell of a lot of things I ain't sure about."

"I'm going to town for my mail." Paddon leaned back

in his chair, eyes showing his uncertainty. "I'd like to stay here. I expect to get word today that construction machinery is being shipped across the Columbia to the mouth of the Deschutes. You're holding the key, Bond. The instant you sign, I'll light out for Triumph and wire our office in Portland. Then we'll start the dirt moving."

Again Clay felt the sense of pressure, the hurry-hurry spirit that possessed this country. He said, "You're welcome to stay here, Paddon," and left the house. He understood the difference between his feelings and those of the people who had lived here, Vicky and Hale and Cotter and the rest. He had been away, but time was running out for those who had been here and had seen railroad rumor after rumor die, leaving only disappointment in their hearts. Now it seemed that steel would come at last, and he was standing in the way. He caught up his roan, saddled him, and mounted. After the horse had unwound in his usual morning buck, and was done, he turned him into the road that cut through the alfalfa and started the long climb.

The sun was only then showing above the rim; the air was still harboring the night chill, and Clay shivered involuntarily. Below him the river made a long silver bow around the bench, bright with the morning sunlight upon it; but shadows clung tenaciously to the east side of the canyon that lifted in staggered rises as it swept away from the narrow bottom.

He stopped often to blow his horse, for the climb was steep, and he felt no need of haste. When he reined up, he would hip around in the saddle and stare below him, subdued by this country, the size and sweep of it, and perhaps by its future. That was it, he knew. His father had talked often of what lay ahead. Now, strangely enough, Sid Starr's daughter had that same dream.

It was midmorning when he rode into the Triangle S

yard and racked his horse. He had never been here before. When he had left, no Bond had been welcome on Sid Starr's range. He knew he would be today. At least, he thought wryly, until the right-of-way agreement was signed.

The ranch was much as he had pictured it—a tall, square house, its white paint making it a landmark for miles around, the big barns and pole corrals and sheds. Here was wealth and power, efficiency and worth, a sense of solidness that made him feel Triangle S would be here long after he was gone. Yet he knew it was a false promise. Mulehide Cotter had said the night before that when the railroad came Triangle S was done, and Vicky was doing her best to bring the railroad. That, to Clay Bond's way of thinking, made less than sense.

.He stepped up on the porch and knocked. No answer. He knocked again, harder, but there was only silence. He turned away, wondering whether to wait, and then saw her ride around the barn and step down. She waved and called, "Good morning, Clay."

He said, "Morning, Vicky," and walked toward her, thinking that Sid Starr was probably turning over in his grave. Vicky stripped gear from her horse and came toward him in her graceful, quick-moving way, her full red lips holding a friendly smile.

"I hear you had some fun last night," she said as she came up to him.

"It wasn't fun for a while." He kicked at a rock, finding this hard to say. Then he blurted, "Thanks for saving our hides. If you hadn't sent your boys over, our goose would have been cooked right and proper."

"It's the least I could do after what you did for me, Clay." She put a hand on his arm and turned him toward the house. "I expected something of the sort, knowing Bronc Main and Dagget. Hugh Kyle's the one I'm not sure about. A railroad fight's a bitter thing. He and Paddon have been at it before, you know."

"Paddon doesn't think it was Kyle's idea."

"He wouldn't. He and Kyle are what you might call friendly enemies, but it strikes me that an enemy is an enemy."

They crossed the porch and went into the house. She waved toward a leather couch. "Sit down, Clay. I'll see if the coffee's still hot."

He sat down, holding his Stetson awkwardly on his knees. He heard her quick sharp step cross into the kitchen, heard the rattle of stove lids as she dropped wood into the firebox. He looked around the big room, thinking with some bitterness that the spirit of Sid Starr still hovered here. There were deer heads on the wall, the antlers holding an array of guns; bearskins on the floor; a great stone fireplace that took up most of the west end of the room, a row of chipped obsidian glittering as a vagrant ray of sunshine caught it. It was a man's room. Even the vase of hollyhocks on the heavy-legged oak table did not dispel that feeling.

Vicky came back and dropped into a chair. "The fire was almost out."

"I just came over to do a lot of thanking." He reached for tobacco and paper, and then dropped his hand. "I expected to find my place gone to pot. Instead Hungry was holding a new house down, and everything was kept up."

"Go ahead and smoke, Clay." She was watching him, her smile warming her face. "There's nothing to thank me for. Let's forget what's past. Did you sign with Paddon yet?"

He stirred uneasily. He had known it would be this way. It was different from the world that had been fifteen years ago. Strangely enough, he was still living in that old dead world more than this girl who had been here on the

Deschutes all of her life.

"No," he said rebelliously. "No sense holding him off, I reckon. I just don't cotton to being pushed into something."

She sobered. "I can see how it would be. It seems to you that we're all in a hurry, doesn't it?"

He nodded. "A big hurry." He reached again for the makings and rolled a smoke. "Looks like I'm in debt to you for a lot of things. Kind of goes against my grain, you being Sid Starr's daughter."

"You're not in debt to me," she said sharply. "It isn't my fault that Sid Starr was my father. I've tried to—to—well, reduce some of the evil he did. Let's start from today."

He fished a match from his pocket. "I found the graves. Thanks for moving Dad's body."

"It's the way it should be," she said simply.

He raised his eyes to her, finding it hard to remember the suspicions he had held of her. "Cotter tried to tell me last night that the trouble between our outfits was Dad's doing as much as Sid's."

"Mulehide wasn't here at the time. Forget it, Clay. I've tried to do that ever since Dad died. This is my home and my outfit. This is my country, and I'm trying to do something for it." She rose and walked around the table, troubled. "I'd give anything to go back and wipe out what happened, but I can't do that. There's no trouble between us, Clay, so there's no sense in us fighting."

"The hay—"

"It's yours. Use it. Sell it to the railroad graders."

"You spent your money building a house—"

"My father. burned the house that Jim Bond built. I've got to live with myself and with memories I'd like to forget. Can't you understand that?"

He ignored her question. "You told Kyle that the railroad wouldn't keep you from raising cows, but last night

Cotter said it meant the end of Triangle S."

"It will mean the end of what Triangle S has been. I'll sell the land that can be farmed. Some day we'll have water on this flat; but until that time comes it will have to be dry-farmed. I'll go along with the changes that the railroad will bring. With less land, I'll have to raise fewer cattle and better ones. Ship them fat."

"Paddon's talk," Clay said.

She nodded. "Railroad talk, if you want to put it that way; but it makes sense. You're in a better position than I am because you have the water."

He had been holding the cigarette in one hand and the match in the other. Rising, he walked to the fireplace, restlessness building in him. He fired the cigarette, tossed the match into the fireplace, and swung back to face her.

"You want to forget everything, but I can't. I held onto my place for fifteen years, and all the time Sid Starr and then you were using it. Triangle S didn't get that quarter section, but it amounted to the same thing. Fifteen years of free use of land because my father was killed, and you expect me to forget it?"

"So that's it." The warmth fled from her face. "I should have known."

"It's true, isn't it?"

"All right," she said in sudden anger. "It's true, so true that, if you will tell me what the use of your place is worth for fifteen years, I'll make you a check for that amount. Then sell your right of way to Paddon and leave the country. You'll have money, a lot of it. Isn't that what you want?"

Now, meeting her eyes, he knew that it was not what he wanted at all. He knew what he did want, the things he had missed as a boy, the things he had never known as a man. It was Sid Starr that had taken them from him— security, a home, a family, a chance to work and grow with the country. Then another thought struck him. Vicky had not had all those things, either. There never could have been any real love or understanding between her and Sid Starr.

He threw his cigarette into the fireplace and came across the room to her. He had tried to hold to his suspicions of this girl, and he could not. She was like no one else he had ever known, and, because of that, he could not judge her as he judged other women he had met.

"Money's not all I want, Vicky. That's what's the matter with Bronc Main."

Her face was upturned, her red full lips were softly pressed, and when he took her into his arms she came willingly. He kissed her, her arms moving up around his neck, and when she drew her lips from his she still stood close to him, her hair touching his face.

She brushed a rebellious black curl away from her forehead, asking, "Is that what you wanted, Clay?"

He hesitated, uncertain of himself, and because he hesitated she turned away. She asked, "Shall I make out your check?"

He took her arm and pulled her around to face him. "No."

"But you'll be riding on, won't you, Clay?" She held her head high, her pride building a wall between them. "Drifting is all you know, isn't it? You've never stopped long enough to let your roots go down. You don't know what it is to love a country and want to see it grow."

"That's right," he said honestly.

"You're like the rest of them. You'll take all you can get that's free. You'll go to Hugh Kyle, and you'll get his best offer. If Paddon won't match it you'll sell to Kyle."

"You've got me wrong," he said angrily. "I'm staying. What'll I ask Paddon?"

She stood very straight, her pointed little chin high.

"That's entirely up to you, Clay."

"It won't be a dollar like you got."

"I'm sure of that."

He felt the cutting edge of her anger, and he didn't understand what had happened. A moment before, he had possessed something he had long wanted. Now he had lost it, and he didn't know why or how. He said curtly, "I'll sign with Paddon tonight," and picking up his Stetson, left the room.

She stood in the doorway watching him mount and ride away, and it was not until he was lost from sight that she remembered the coffee.

Chapter Twelve: TROUBLE SHOOTER

WALT PADDON RODE IN THAT EVENING with the first shadows gathering along the river. Clay met him as he swung down. He said, "Get out your right-of-way agreements, Paddon. I'm signing."

Paddon watered his horse, eyeing Clay quizzically. "What happened?"

"Nothing," Clay said impatiently. "No use holding things up. I'm ready to sign."

"The price?"

"What's it worth to you?"

"It's worth the fifty thousand you asked," Paddon said frankly. "We both know that. Trouble is, I've got some bosses who hang onto their moneybags with both hands. If this thing goes too high, they'll tighten up, and there won't be any railroad. It'll cost like hell anyhow."

"Quit beating around the bush," Clay said.

Paddon swallowed and kicked at the end of the log trough. "Let me make an offer, Bond. Say, five thousand and a job. You won't need to do any work on your place until spring."

"What kind of a job?"

"There'll be trouble. More trouble than I figured any railroad would have at this day and age. There's no sign of Kyle in Lava City. Dagget's gone. Bronc Main's gone. None of his outfit is in town, and nobody knows where they are. Looks to me like it adds up to trouble. After watching you whittle Dagget down and handle the fight last night, I'm convinced you're my man."

Some of the tension that had been in Clay from the time he had left Triangle S went out of him. He needed a fight, and Paddon was promising him one. He said, "I'm your huckleberry."

"One hundred dollars a week," Paddon said crisply. "We're going to Triumph in the morning. Our first bargeload of machinery has crossed the Columbia. We'll have a dozen camps from here to the mouth of the Deschutes, and we'll build roads from the rim to the river. We'll be moving supplies. We'll be buying cattle to feed our men. There'll be a dozen ways Main can get at us. Your job is to outguess him and stop him."

Clay grinned. "It'll be fun." He jerked his head at the house. "Supper's ready. Go on in soon as you put your horse up."

Clay started toward the corral and swung back when Paddon called, "Where are you going?"

"To Triangle S."

"I thought you went over there this morning."

"I did. I want to see Vicky again."

"Maybe you'd better sign up before you go." Paddon paused, and added significantly, "A dead man willing to sign won't do us much good."

Clay returned to the trough and waited impatiently until Paddon made out the check and handed him the pen and agreement blank. He pocketed the check, signed his name on the line Paddon indicated, and handed the pen and paper back. He said, "Paddon, I keep wondering why Main is against the Oregon Southern as much as he is. I know he's the big duck in the puddle as far as the desert goes, and he figgers a railroad will bring settlers; but that ain't enough to make him pull off a raid like he did last night."

Paddon slapped his reins against his leg, eyeing Clay a moment. Finally he said, "I haven't told this to anyone. Vicky knows it because George Akin told her before he headed into the desert, and I suppose by now Main knows it. The truth is, we intend building across the desert from Lava City to hook up with the railroad at Ontario. The Department of Agriculture has just said the high desert is fit for dry farming. Add those two things up, Bond, and you get ten thousand settlers who'll swarm all over Main's range."

It added up, all right, and for the first time Clay understood the desperate position in which Main had been placed by the rush of events. He asked, "If he's cornered like that, why is he buying over here on the river?"

Paddon shrugged. "Who knows how a man like Main figures? Maybe he aims to hit back at Vicky. Or maybe he thinks he can block us. Anyhow, this is a better place to winter his stock than the desert."

Clay, remembering the Flying M owner, could see how it was. Bronc Main would go on expanding until he was finished, for he was not a man who would consider the possibility of defeat.

"I'll be ready to go, come sunup. Tell Hungry."

Quickly Clay saddled his roan and, mounting, rode out of the canyon. He did not take the leisurely pace of that morning, for now the need to see Vicky was a burning necessity in him. All afternoon the memory of her kiss had been a sweet haunting reminder that he loved her. He had tried to hold himself away from her since he had first met her at Benton's roadhouse; he had kept alive his old hatred of the name Starr, and he had let that hatred feed his suspicions of her. Now he understood how completely wrong he had been. He had surrendered, unequivocally, and he had to tell her.

He came out of the canyon, dark now with evening shadow, and kept his roan at a fast pace. The last of the day's sunlight was still bright here on the rolling plateau, and ahead of him rimrock made a sharp break across the face of the flat. Between him and the broken country was land that could be dry-farmed, land that Sid Starr had claimed for a generation. Now for the first time, he began to understand how much Vicky's devotion to an ideal was costing her.

Plans formed in Clay's mind as he rode. There was no vacillation in him now. He had made his choice, and there would be no turning back. This would be his home, his country, and he would grow with it. He had his dreams, and Vicky was the center of them. His roots would go down with hers. His aimless drifting, embittered by boyhood memories, was behind him, and he was glad he was back. He wanted her to know that.

The Cascades hid the sun, and dusk darkened the sage flat as if a steadily thickening blue veil had been spread upon it. Rimrock dropped into purple dimness and was lost against the horizon, and the smell of dust was heavy in the evening air. Ahead of him lamps bloomed behind the windows of the Triangle S buildings. Then he was there, racking his horse. He turned up the path, vaguely aware of talk flowing from the bunkhouse.

She must have heard him coming, for she was there on the porch, standing slim and straight, a shapely silhouette against the lamplight. She said, "You're back."

"Couldn't stay away." He put his hands on her arms and felt her tremble. "I done it. I've got Paddon's check, and he's got my signed agreement. You'll have your railroad."

"I guess I'm supposed to thank you."

"I've got a job with him," he hurried on. "Sort of a trouble shooter. I'm supposed to keep Main and his bunch from doing anything that'll stop construction. It'll be fun."

"Shooting fun," she said, her voice frigidly distant.

"I'll leave Hungry on the place to keep an eye on things. I'll work until Paddon doesn't need me. Then we'll make something out of the place. I've got a better idea than Paddon's notion of feeding cattle and shipping. We'll raise blooded stuff, the best whitefaces I can buy. These farmers coming in will need stock, and I'll have it to sell them."

"Sounds fine."

He put his arms around her and brought her to him and kissed her. She was passive, not fighting but giving him nothing. Her lips were still under his kiss. Puzzled, he let her go.

For a moment she stood looking at him, her face composed. Then she asked, "Did you ever kiss a woman seriously, Clay?"

He stared at her, not understanding. Without another word she whirled and ran into the house. He stood rooted there, hearing her steps cross the big living-room, heard a door slam. He started after her, calling, "Vicky!"

Then he stopped, for Mulehide Cotter stood by the oak table, a cocked gun in his hand, his square-jawed face frankly hostile. He said, "You're a fool, Bond, a damned, bungling fool. Get this straight. If you come around here again and hurt Vicky, I'll kill you. Now get out."

Clay took a long breath, knowing that fighting Cotter would injure Vicky more than anything he had already unwittingly done. He turned and strode back to his horse. Mounting, he rode away, the eagerness that he had felt a moment before completely gone. In its place puzzlement and hurt were a misery in him.

Chapter Thirteen: KYLE'S OFFER

CLAY AND PADDON RODE out of the canyon at dawn, the sky steel-gray. Then they topped the east rim and saw the sun, its light sharp upon the land. They angled to the northeast, reached the road within the hour, and turned toward the Columbia, passing within a mile of the Triangle S buildings.

"I wish I knew what Main and Dagget are up to," Paddon said worriedly. "Kyle's probably signing up right-of-way agreements, but it isn't like Main to drop out of sight."

"The high desert is big enough to swallow an army," Clay said.

Paddon shook his head. "He can't hit us from out there. It strikes me that he's likely to make his big play now. Give me a month, Bond, and nobody'll stop us; but if expenses and trouble roll up now, we're finished before we start."

"I thought this George Akin that Vicky was trying to find was a big gun in the company, and he wanted the road built."

"If he was in my place he'd build this road, come hell or high water," Paddon said; "but a dead man can't build a railroad. If I fail, I'll be afraid to meet Akin in the hereafter." He stared at a notch in the rimrock ahead of them. "George never failed at anything he set out to do if he figured it would make the world a better place to live in. It would be a hell of a thing if the job he died for was never done."

That was a new thought to Clay Bond. He had seen dozens of men meet violent deaths of one sort or another, but few of them had died to make the world a better place. If George Akin was dead, that would be the reason for his dying; it would be the same if Walt Paddon died engineering a railroad up the Deschutes. Then he thought of Vicky Starr. He had thought of her every waking moment, it seemed, since he had kissed her yesterday morning. He had gained her love and he had lost it, and he had not known why. Now he thought he did.

Vicky had considered him as a man returning to a boyhood home that would be entirely changed by the railroad, and she had credited him with both the willingness and the ability to grow with the country. Yesterday he had forced her to reverse her judgment because he had shown her how much his suspicions and old hatreds had bound his thinking. She had done what she could to help him rise above those hatreds, but it had not been enough. In making her final judgment, she had seen him as a man trying to squeeze what he could from a situation which favored him, a situation which he deserved no credit for creating.

Vicky Starr had been thinking in terms of what was good for the country; he had been thinking in terms of what was good for Clay Bond. He knew he could never give her up, and he knew, too, that the change which had come in him was due to her. Somehow he must make her see that he had caught the same vision she had. He had to prove to her that his real reason for signing on with Paddon was to build a railroad, that the hundred dollars a week was the lesser thing.

They crossed Buck Creek valley, climbed the steep, twisting passage that was Cow Canyon, and came out upon bleak Triumph Flats. Here the endless miles were carpeted thinly by bunch grass and stunted sagebrush, a country that would never be good for anything but grazing. It was a motionless land unchanged by time; it would look the same in ten years or fifty years, regardless of the steel rails that were to be pushed up the Deschutes canyon far below them to the west.

"A damned poor piece of earth," Paddon muttered. "Triumph ships more wool than any other town in the country; but, when you've said that, you've said it all."

They rode into Triumph as the first evening shadows flowed across the flat. It was a larger town than Clay had expected to see, throbbing with the primitive beat of frontier life. Warehouses and shipping corrals lay along the track. Business blocks were strung haphazardly to the west —Main Street, lined with stables, stores, eating-places, and saloons. This was the end of steel for the rich hinterland that stretched far to the south, the railhead for the treasure chest that was central Oregon.

Progress had flowed westward along the Columbia to the Willamette valley because the Columbia gorge furnished the only water grade by which a railroad could cross the Cascades. So the railroad magnates had decreed that western Oregon would develop, that central Oregon would remain untouched. This tiny spur, reaching southward to Triumph, was only a ridiculous beginning at the job which must be done.

"Why don't Kyle's bunch run their line south from here?" Clay asked.

"Too steep a grade coming up from the Columbia," Paddon answered as they turned into Main Street. "The Deschutes is the only answer." He laughed softly. "Akin wrote that the canyon was a tunnel with the top off. That's just about it."

They reined into a stable and left the horses with instructions for their care, then crossed the street to the Triumph Hotel, angling around a settler's covered wagon that was slowly wheeling southward.

"I keep a room here all the time," Paddon said. "Have

to if I want to be sure of a bed. People are moving in like it was a gold rush. That's what a little railroad talk does."

When they had finished supper in the hotel dining-room Clay asked, "What do I do to earn my wages?"

"Keep your eyes and ears open," Paddon said. "Make a round of the saloons. It's my guess that this is where we'll have trouble. We'll start construction at the mouth of the Deschutes, but we'll also ship machinery and supplies to Triumph and freight them down to the bottom of the canyon. That means we'll have to build wagon roads to the river. In other words, we'll lay steel at a dozen different places at the same time, so we'll be moving a hell of a lot faster than if we had to depend on our new line to do our hauling."

Clay sensed the urgency that was growing in Paddon. He said, "Suppose I run into Dagget or Kyle?"

"Just listen. I want to know what we're up against." Paddon glanced at his watch. "I'm dog-tired, but I've got to see a man about a warehouse. We'll have grub piled up here along the tracks in three days." He struck the table with the palm of his hand. "Damn it, I've got to wire the Portland office. Almost forgot to let them know you'd signed." He grinned. "You weren't aware of it, but the eyes of the railroad world have been on you."

Clay pushed back his chair and rose. "Well, they can shut their eyes now. I'll look into the saloons and go to bed."

He found no trace of the men he sought. He went to bed and dropped at once into a dreamless sleep, not even waking when Paddon came in at midnight. It was after seven the next morning when he woke. Paddon lay on his side, snoring loudly. Clay remained motionless for a time, staring at the dirty wallpaper on the ceiling, sunlight a sharp line around the green shade. He found himself thinking of Vicky Starr, a vague uneasiness working in him. It might be months before he would see her again.

Throwing back the covers, he climbed out of bed without waking Paddon. He raised the shade, shaved, and dressed, and was buckling his gun belt on when Paddon woke.

Paddon knuckled his eyes and yawned. "Must be almost sunup."

"It's after eight. Aiming to sleep all day?"

"Not till after the railroad's built." Paddon swung his feet to the floor. "I got the warehouse signed up. Kyle slipped on that. I was afraid he'd have everything leased." He yawned again. "Trouble with Kyle's bunch is that they don't want to waste any money until they know for sure we're going to build. Now they'll bust their buttons off."

"I'm going down for a bait of ham and eggs."

Paddon nodded. "Go ahead." He watched Clay cross the room to the door. "Bond, it's my guess you'll see Kyle today. He'll ask if you've signed up."

"What'll I tell him?"

"Tell him you've signed with me. Then he'll want to buy a right of way across your place to parallel ours. Let him have it." Paddon scratched his stubble-covered chin. "Then, if I read Kyle right, you'll get an offer to double-cross us. That's the difference between him and me. He figures anybody can be reached by money."

There was an unspoken question in his words, a final challenge of Clay's loyalty. Anger stirred briefly in Clay and died. The game was bigger than he had realized at first, so big that a double cross on his part would be a crippling blow to the Oregon Southern. Now, perfectly honest with himself, he mentally admitted that he had yet to prove his loyalty to Walt Paddon.

"Let's get one thing straight," he said evenly. "When I first hit Lava City, I'd have sold out to the highest bidder. I won't now. Vicky is to blame for that."

"I knew you wouldn't," Paddon said quickly, his face showing he sensed his mistake.

Clay left the room, closing the door behind him. He went down the twisting stairs to the dining-room, had breakfast, and stepped into the street. In broad daylight the town showed a tawdry transient quality that had been hidden by the night. Within a few years Triumph would be a ghost town, the excuse for its existence gone. Trains hauling the bulky wealth of the interior would roar northward down the Deschutes, and Triumph, by-passed by the main line, would crumble into decay as a thousand other end-of-steel towns had done in the past.

He had a smoke, loitering in front of the hotel as he watched the milling crowd of stockmen, settlers, gamblers, land locators, and bunco artists. Again he was surprised at the feeling of expectancy that lay upon the town. He had had some of that feeling in Lava City, but it was more noticeable here, for Triumph was the jumping-off place. Some were honestly seeking a chance to work and profit by the opportunities a railroad would bring, others were here to prey upon those who had money; but all held one thing in common, a feeling that the end of the rainbow lay to the south, and the pot of gold was waiting there for them.

Finishing the cigarette, Clay flipped the stub into the street, paused until a jerk-line freight outfit rolled by, and crossed the dust strip to Clancy's Bar, the biggest saloon in town. He asked for beer and stood with a foot on the brass rail, waiting. He had let himself be seen. If Kyle was in town he'd show up.

Clay didn't wait long. Kyle sauntered in, very casually as if for no purpose except to have a drink. Clay played the same game, giving no indication that he was aware of the Columbia & Cascade man's presence. Kyle walked up to the bar. He said, "Howdy, Pat," and cuffed his hat back.

He called for whisky, and then apparently saw Clay for the first time.

"Why, howdy, Bond," Kyle said jovially. "Didn't see you. When did you ride in?"

"Last night."

Kyle picked up his bottle and glass and moved along the mahogany to stand beside Clay. "Glad to see you again, Bond. I had thought of riding down to your place, but didn't know whether you were there or not."

"I've been there, but I had a hell of a time staying," Clay said pointedly.

"Heard you had a gun ruckus. What was it about?"

"You know damned well. It was Lew Dagget leading Main's bunch."

"Why should I know?" Kyle asked.

Anger began working in Clay. He had none of Paddon's feeling that Kyle had no part in the raid, that his way would be legal trickery and not violence.

"Don't try play-acting with me, Kyle," he said hotly. "If I got rubbed out before I signed with Paddon, the Oregon Southern would have a hell of a time getting a right of way across my place and up Buck Creek, wouldn't it?"

The twitch at the corners of Kyle's mouth was a signal that rashness was crowding him; but he held his voice even. "You're wrong on two counts, Bond. In the first place, the Oregon Southern could eventually condemn a right of way. In the second place, neither me nor my company play the game with murder."

Clay waved the railroad man's words away. "Condemning a right of way takes money and time, and the Oregon Southern is ready to build now. As for you not playing the game with murder, I say you're talking hogwash. Looked to me that day in Lava City that you and Dagget and Main were all playing the same tune."

"Main's a cowman," Kyle said with unnecessary belligerence. "I'm a railroad man. Why should we play the same tune?"

"You don't want to build unless you have to, and Main don't want a railroad because it'll bring settlers pouring onto his range. Don't take no big brain to figger out that you've thrown in together."

Kyle shrugged as if realizing he had boxed himself in. He turned the empty glass with the tips of his stubby fingers, flinty eyes pinned on Clay's face. Finally he said, "Bond, you can add it up any way you damn please. Main's got his game. I'm playing the Columbia & Cascade's." He drew a pen and checkbook from his pocket and laid them on the bar. "Did you sign with Paddon?"

"Yes."

"I supposed you would. Now, listen, Bond. What happens to a bunch of clodbusters or some fool optimist who files on a timber claim thinking he'll have a railroad and a sawmill is no affair of yours. This is your chance to make your stake, and you'd be a fool if you didn't grab it. There's a lot of visionary talk going around about developing the country. That's Vicky Starr's line, but I take you for a hardheaded businessman."

He paused, eyes narrowing as he waited for Clay's reaction.

Clay said, "Keep talking."

"Your signing with Paddon don't keep you from letting us have a right of way across your place." Kyle tapped his checkbook. "We'll pay well. Say, ten thousand. How does that figure sound?"

"Sounds too damned good. You've got a joker in your deck, Kyle. Turn it over."

Kyle reached into his pocket for a cigar. "There is one small angle I didn't mention. You're with Paddon, aren't you?"

Clay nodded. "I'm on his payroll."

Kyle's blocky face was softened by a small smile. "That's fine, Bond; but when luck has dropped a fortune into a man's lap like she has yours there's no reason why you shouldn't be on two payrolls. It isn't often that circumstances make a quarter section as valuable as they have yours."

"I'm still listening."

Kyle reached for the whisky bottle and poured himself another drink. Clay felt the hesitation in him. The man wasn't sure he had read Clay right; but he would make his try, because he went on the basis that anybody could be reached by money.

"Give this careful thought before you make a decision," Kyle went on in his persuasive tone. "My ten thousand dollars plus what you have from Paddon will add up to a nice chunk of cash. There's nothing to be gained from nursing another man's cows for thirty a month and beans. Here's your chance to get your own spread."

"You're sure chasing your rabbit around the bush," Clay said impatiently.

"I want to be sure you don't go off halfcocked. Here's my proposition. Paddon likely carries the agreement you signed in his pocket. Chances are he has Vicky Starr's. Get those and bring them to me. Sign a right-of-way agreement for me, and the ten thousand is yours."

"I never go off halfcocked," Clay breathed. "Likewise I never sell a man out when I hire on with him."

He hit Kyle on the side of the head, a hard right that started below his waist. Kyle had time to duck or drive a fist at him, but did neither. Clay's reaction must have stunned him, for he stood there as if paralyzed, seeing the blow coming and doing nothing.

The sound of fist on bone was a meaty thud that flowed across the big room. Kyle spun and fell. Clay stood over him, waiting, but Kyle made no effort to get back on his feet. He stared up at Clay, dazed, one hand rubbing the side of his face. That was when Dagget and Main's crew piled into the room.

They came through the back, ten of them. Dagget bawled, "There he is, boys. Work him over."

They were on Clay before he had time to draw his gun. He struck out, knocked one man back into the others, flattened a nose, and brought a rush of blood; but there were too many of them. He went down under their great weight, kicked, and tried to roll; but there was nothing he could do. They had made their plans carefully and well. Two men grabbed his legs, two more his arms, and held him on the floor so that only his head could move.

He stared up at Dagget, seeing the malicious triumph on the man's muscle-ridged face. This was murder, coldly planned so that Lew Dagget could enjoy each second that it took to kill him.

Kyle shook his head and got to his feet. Leaning against the bar, he said thickly, "Stop it, Dagget."

Apparently Dagget didn't hear. He rubbed his right fist into the palm of his left hand, yellow eyes mocking. "You're mighty damned tough, ain't you, Bond? Cut quite a swath since you got back. Well, you'll find things ain't changed much. I used to work for Starr. Now it's Main. Same proposition."

"Call your wolves off, Dagget," Clay shouted in frantic rage. "I licked you in Lava City. I can do it in Triumph."

"Haul him up, boys," Dagget said coldly. "He wants to lick me."

The men holding Clay's feet moved back. He was jerked upright, the other two still gripping his wrists behind him. Dagget stepped forward, right fist still rubbing his left palm, a sadistic grin curling thick lips. He lashed out at Clay's jaw. Stars pinwheeled before Clay's vision; but he wouldn't beg, and there was no use to ask again for a fair fight. Dagget had had his fair fight, and he'd failed. He wouldn't risk it a second time.

Clay's head rang with the blow. Dagget struck him again, and his legs gave with the weight. One of the men holding him kneed him in the back, growling, "Stand up." Through the ringing in his ears he heard Kyle's voice pleading, "Stop it, Dagget."

Dagget brought his fist back for another blow. Clay saw the tiny red specks in the man's yellow eyes, saw the wet shine of his brown lips. He kicked out with both feet, sagging in the hands of the men who held his arms. His spike heels dug into Dagget's protuberant belly, driving wind and a smothered oath out of him.

A gun barked from the batwings. Dagget grabbed his left arm and reeled against the mahogany. Paddon said evenly, "You boys holding Bond let go. Next time I'm putting my bullets into your briskets."

The men let Clay go and spun toward the batwings. He fell, got to hands and knees, and struggled upright. He pulled gun, knowing Paddon would need help. This wasn't his game. The men before Clay seemed to be twins, the outlines of their bodies blurred.

"Git," Clay said. "Out through the front."

He held the gun steady, masking his weakness. Paddon stepped away from the door, motioning with his left hand. "I'm giving you five seconds, Dagget. If you've got any sense, you'll never show your ugly mug around here again."

Blood was seeping through the fingers of Dagget's right hand. He threw a quick glance at Kyle, saw no help there, and started for the door. As he passed Paddon he said, "You're licked, mister. Akin'll pull you off."

"Akin!" Paddon cried. "Where is he?"

Dagget did not answer. He went outside, his men streaming behind him. A moment later they were in saddles and pounding south. Clay swung to the bar and poured himself a drink. He wiped a hand across his bruised face.

"That's one way to lick a man." Clay felt gingerly of his face again and added, "Thanks, Paddon."

"I was watching from the hotel," Paddon said. "I saw Kyle come in. Then Dagget's bunch rode up, Dagget looked over the batwings, and they all went around back. I waited a minute, figuring I'd better let Kyle have plenty of time, but looks like I waited too long."

Clay's vision had cleared. He pinned his eyes on Kyle. "No, you did it just right, Paddon. Kyle here had a right funny notion." He told Paddon about Kyle's offer and asked, "Why would he want Vicky's agreement stolen? She could always sign another one."

"Wait a minute." Paddon grabbed his arm. "Maybe they aim to fix it so she couldn't."

Kyle started backing away along the bar. Clay drew his gun and laid it on the mahogany. He said, "Stand pat, Kyle, and start talking."

Kyle licked trembling lips. "I don't know anything about it."

Clay picked up his gun. "I'll shoot him in the right elbow. Then the left. Then his wrists. He'll be in a hell of a shape, Paddon."

"I've fought you from here to hell-an'-gone, Kyle," Paddon raged, "but I never figured you were the kind who'd tie up with coyotes like Dagget and Main."

Clay eared back the hammer of his gun. "Right elbow first."

"Don't let him, Walt," Kyle screamed. "Don't let him."

Paddon's lips curled in contempt. "Why should I stop him?"

Kyle lurched toward Clay. "I tell you I didn't know anything about Dagget being in town. I didn't have anything to do with them holding you and beating you. All I know is that Main's holding George Akin. He's got him on the Flying M."

"You sure that's all?" Clay demanded.

Kyle licked dry lips. "There is one more thing. It's Main's idea, so I don't know just what he's up to, but he's figuring on sending Vicky Starr word that Akin wants to see her."

Clay wheeled on Paddon. "He's tricking Vicky into coming out there. They'll kill her, and nobody'll ever know what happened to her. That's why Kyle wanted me to steal her right-of-way agreement."

"I tell you I don't know what Main's up to," Kyle cried.

White-faced, Paddon said, "Dagget aimed to kill you, too. Then they'd really have us sewed up."

Clay holstered his gun. "Kyle, you'd better tell your company to send in another man. You're finished." He motioned to Paddon. "You can take me off your payroll. From here on out I'm playing my own game."

He strode out of the saloon, Paddon running to keep up with him. "What's the idea, telling me to take you off the payroll?"

"I'm going after Vicky. I don't expect to find your man Akin alive. That makes this job my business, not the Oregon Southern's."

"Going after Vicky is Oregon Southern's business, my friend," Paddon said sharply. "You're staying on the payroll. Don't you forget it."

Clay stopped and faced him, the noon-high sun beating down upon them. "I thought railroads weren't interested in anything but paying the stockholders dividends."

A small smile touched Paddon's lips. "Railroads belong to corporations, and corporations do not have souls. Our enemies like to say that, and it's true; but our enemies forget one thing. The men who work for the railroads do have souls. We don't forget our friends, and Vicky Starr is the best friend we have." He held out his hand. "Good luck, son."

Clay shook hands and strode on toward the livery stable. He had been telling himself he must convince Vicky that he saw this railroad business the same way she did, that what was past was past and their lives were their own to live regardless of what had happened between their fathers. But those things which had been so important in his thoughts a few minutes before had lost their significance. Just one thing was important—he had to catch Vicky before she got to the Flying M.

Chapter Fourteen: MESSAGE FROM JASON WADE

VICKY WAS NOT SURE when she realized she was in love with Clay Bond. Perhaps it had been the first time he kissed her. Or maybe it had been before that.

She would never forget the long hours of waiting after her crew had ridden out, headed for the Bond place, the fear that had clung to her until her stomach felt as if she had swallowed a huge ball of ice that refused to melt. Nor would she forget the weakness of relief that made her knees feel like rubber when they returned and she ran out of the house and Mulehide Cotter called to her, "Everything's all right, Vicky. They high-tailed like rabbits with a bee sitting on 'em."

Clay had come the next morning as she had been sure he would. She had let him kiss her, and she had kissed him, the kind of kiss she had never given another man. At the moment she had not understood why she felt the way she did, all feather-light with angels singing to her. As she thought about it now, it seemed crazy and fantastic. Just that one moment. No more, for she had drawn her head back to ask, "Is that what you wanted, Clay?" *He had not answered!*

Crazy, completely crazy to think so much of a man that, when he hesitated, she felt as if he had torn her heart out. The feather-lightness was gone; the angels stopped singing. She had been so sure he would say, "That's everything I want. I love you." But he hadn't. He hadn't said anything.

He'd just stood looking at her, his wind-burned face showing no expression that she could identify. She didn't know why he had kissed her unless it was to prove to himself that he could kiss Sid Starr's daughter. Or perhaps he rode around kissing every girl he could. There was one thing that seemed to be certain. He had not been close to telling her he loved her.

If he just hadn't stood there, acting as if it meant nothing to him at all. If he had even wanted to kiss her again. Or if he had said something to show he had any feeling in him. She had tried to make her kiss tell him how she felt; but he hadn't understood—or, if he had, it had meant nothing. Maybe he had ridden back to the river and bragged to Hungry Hale that Vicky Starr was soft. All he had to do was to kiss her, and she was as easy to shape as warm butter.

It was a long time since Vicky Starr had cried over anything, but she had cried that afternoon. She hadn't been sure why except that now nothing seemed important. She didn't care whether she lived through the day or not. She had thought her fight for the railroad was big and worth while. Now it seemed as if it were only a two-bit ruckus over whether ties and rails were to be laid across a sagebrush flat.

Nothing would make any difference to her. She'd be an old maid. She'd never kiss another man. She'd never have a family of her own. She'd be a man-woman doing a man's work. In a final burst of temper she told herself that if

Clay Bond ever showed his face on the Triangle S again she'd fill his hide full of buckshot.

But he had come back, and she hadn't thought of the shotgun. She had waited on the porch, hoping he would come, and when she had first heard his horse off across the flat her heart had pounded so hard she could hardly breathe. She had been certain it was Clay. Then she had let herself act the fool.

Thinking back over it now, she could not understand why she had done what she had. It was a sudden and quite unexplainable fit of perverseness that had made her fail to respond to his kiss. She had supposed he would return, very humble, and say he loved her so much that railroads and cows and fathers who had fought didn't mean a thing. Instead he had talked about getting Paddon's check and a job and raising blooded stock.

She had let herself ask the question, "Did you ever kiss a woman seriously, Clay?" Again he could have said, "I just kissed you seriously. I love you." But no, he'd stood there staring at her as if he didn't know what she was talking about. So she had run from him. If she had stayed she would have cried; and she was too proud to let him see her tears.

She slept very little that night. From her bedroom window she watched the sun tip up over the Blue Mountains, watched the night retreat until the last of the shadows were gone and the sage flat became a vast gray sea in the early-morning light.

Vicky had often stood here at the window and watched the sun come up. In the weird indistinctness of dawn, she had superimposed a dream above reality. In her mind she had seen irrigation ditches running between alfalfa fields, she had seen the houses and barns of the settlers, and she had heard the shrill whistle of a locomotive swelling across the flat. But this morning the dream would not come. She saw a sage flat, no more, no less; and that was probably what it would remain.

She heard the talk of men at the corrals and knew the crew was saddling up. She left the house, telling herself she should know where they were going, but at the same time knowing that she was prompted by the simple urge to talk to someone. By the time she reached the yard between the house and corrals, the men had mounted; but Cotter saw her and motioned for the crew to wait.

"Where are you going?" Vicky asked as she came up to Cotter.

"Pigeon Creek. Thought we'd better see how the grass was."

"You'll be back tonight?"

Cotter hesitated, shifting uneasily in the saddle as he looked away from her. "I ain't real sure."

She sensed that there was more to this than he had said. The men all carried Colts in their holsters and Winchesters in the scabbards. She said tartly, "Looks like you're going to see how the grass is by staring down the barrel of a Colt."

"Might as well tell you," Cotter said. "We've been missing a few steers. I've got a hunch Bronc Main is taking 'em just to rawhide us, or maybe he's fixing to make a real haul. Anyhow, I'm taking the sheriff with me to help me look, and before we're done I've got a notion we'll pay the Flying M a visit."

"It's not worth getting killed over," she said.

Cotter motioned for his men to ride on. He rolled a smoke, his eyes on Vicky, his tough, scarred face filled with concern. Finally he said, "We've come a long ways together, Vicky. I hate to see it blow up in smoke. Trouble is, you never know what's in the head of a man like Bronc Main; but after the meeting in Lava City and the scrap at Bond's place I've got a hunch that Bronc's fixing to move in on us."

Looking at Cotter, she saw the feeling he had for her. She had sensed it before, and she wondered if she could ever love him. He had given her all the loyalty a man could ever give a woman. Actually it was more than loyalty. He was steadfast. That was the word to describe him, she told herself. It was a quality that had meant a great deal to her, for she would have been lonely without him and the knowledge that he was always there.

"It won't blow up in smoke," she said, "no matter how many railroads we have on the Deschutes or what Bronc Main plans to do. He may be king of the desert, but he's not king on the river." Spontaneously she raised a hand to his arm. "I've never thanked you for all the things you've done for me. I don't have the words to thank you, but it's meant so much."

His face turned red, for he was not a man to talk about his feelings nor to analyze them. He said gruffly, "No thanks coming my way. It's this Clay Bond I'm wondering about. I'm thinking you're beginning to like him, and I don't figger he's the right man for you. Look at the mess he's kicked up."

"The mess was ready to be kicked," she said warmly. "It'll take some more kicking as long as Bronc Main's alive."

"I aim to use the toe of my boot today," Cotter said, and rode away.

She stood in the bright morning sunlight watching Cotter and the others until they dropped down into a dry wash and were lost to sight. From somewhere off to her right a meadow lark burst into song. On any other day she would have thought it was the most beautiful sound on earth, but today she was hardly aware of it. She was thinking of Mulehide Cotter and the look on his face. He loved her, but he would never speak of it. As long as she wanted him or needed him, he would be here.

"Steadfast!" She said the word aloud, and her thoughts turned to Clay Bond and became bitter. It was a strange trick that Fate had played on her. Cotter loved her, and she loved Clay. And Clay? Probably he didn't love anybody. He had been a drifter, and it was unlikely that he would ever change. He had said he was staying, but a few months of hard work would change him. She knew the kind.

She returned to the house and built a fire in the kitchen. She got out the frying-pan and a side of bacon and then put them away. It would be a waste to cook breakfast for herself this morning. She made coffee, idling by the stove until it was done, and then brought a cup from the pantry and filled it. She tried to drink it, but there was no taste to it; so she poured it back and moved the pot to the back of the stove.

Vicky's days were never long enough to do the things she wanted to do, but today time dragged. There seemed to be nothing to do. She thought of making a cake and decided she didn't have the patience. She took out her sewing and put it away. The last piece of poplin she had bought at Old Peter's was still untouched, but this was not the day to work on it.

She went into the front room and looked around, dissatisfaction growing in her. It was still Sid Starr's room. Except for the hollyhocks on the table, the room was exactly the same as when he had died. She could not explain to herself why she had left everything this way when she had tried so hard to make Triangle S mean the opposite to what her father had made it. It was, she supposed, a sort of memorial to him.

Walking around the room, she looked at the guns and bearskins and the cavernous fireplace, and it struck her that she had not hated her father so much as she had thought. There were many things about him she had admired. It was just that he had set his sights on the wrong thing. Her mother had died a long time ago. If she had lived Sid Starr's later years might have been very different. Many times he had told Vicky that she was exactly like her mother.

Outside a man called, "Hello, the house."

Vicky had not seen anyone ride up. She hurried out, seeing that this man was a stranger in his middle thirties with a flaring yellow mustache and black beady eyes that were touched by desire as they swept her small trim body. She stopped, not liking it, and instinctively warned by some quality she sensed in the man. Except for the cook she was alone.

"You Vicky Starr?" the man asked.

"Yes."

He fumbled in his shirt pocket and pulled out a folded sheet of paper. "Got a letter from Jason Wade for you. Told me it was worth five dollars if I delivered it to you personally. Of course, I could have stuck the dinero into my pocket and kept going; but I'm an honest man, lady, so here it is."

She took it, said, "Thanks," and, turning, walked rapidly to the house.

The man sat his saddle, gaze following her. Then he saw the cook standing in the door of the cookshack. Shrugging, the man rode around the house and headed north.

Vicky did not stop to read the letter until she saw the stranger ride on. She was seldom afraid of anyone, but this stranger worried her. She never trusted a man who felt that he must speak of his own honesty. When he had gone she drew the letter from the envelope and unfolded it. The writing was Wade's. She had seen it before, and she was sure he had written this, for it was not a handwriting that would be easy to forge.

Dear Vicky,

Cash Taber has just brought word to me that George Akin is alive, but he isn't well. Taber says that Akin wants to see you at once. I didn't believe Taber, so he's taking me to the Flying M to prove that he isn't lying. I'll try to get Akin to tell me what he wants to tell you, but he may refuse. I realize that he trusted you more than any of the rest of us, so if you're willing to take the risk of going out there to see him, I suggest that you be in Lava City when I come back. If it's necessary for you to see Akin, I'll go with you.

Your fellow laborer for a railroad,
Jason Wade

When Vicky had left Benton's roadhouse she had given up the idea of trying to find Akin herself; but apparently Main had changed his mind about allowing her to come to the Flying M, or Taber wouldn't have come for Wade. She could not doubt Wade's integrity. On the other hand, he was a new man in the country, and he would not understand Bronc Main. There was a chance he was being fooled.

She was aware this might be a trap, but she could not let Akin down if he honestly wanted to see her. She went upstairs and changed to riding-clothes. Fifteen minutes later she was riding south toward Lava City.

Chapter Fifteen: BRONC MAIN'S MOVE

CLAY HELD HIS ROAN to a fast pace when he left Triumph, but it was dark before he reached Triangle S. The only light about the place was in the cookshack, and when he called, "Hello, the house," it went out. There was a moment of silence, then the squeak of an opening door.

"Who is it?" a man asked.

"Clay Bond. Where is everybody?"

The man said nothing for a time. A sense that something was wrong slid into Clay. Dismounting, he moved noiselessly away from his horse so that he stood with his back against a poplar tree. He couldn't see the other man, for there was no moon and the stars were veiled by a thick overcast; but he judged that the fellow was standing against the cookshack wall, hesitant to speak because he would give his position away.

"The boys are in the high country," the man said at last, "and Vicky's in Lava City."

If the man had refused to speak, Clay would have been certain he was an enemy. Now he wasn't sure. He asked, "Who are you?"

"The cook."

It might be true. Still, the man had been too careful when he rode up. "I just got in from Triumph. How about some grub?"

"Sorry, but I'm plumb out of everything. Vicky's bringing a load of supplies from town."

Then Clay knew that things were not right. A cook for an outfit the size of Triangle S could always find something to eat. This man, then, must belong to Dagget's bunch. Panic rushed through Clay. Where was Vicky, and where were the real cook and the Triangle S hands? And how many more of Dagget's outfit were around?

"I'm plumb lank." Clay knew he had to force this until the other broke. "I've got to have something to eat."

"Sorry," the man said curtly. "You can eat in Lava City."

Clay drew his Colt, and the instant it cleared leather he heard the click of another gun being brought to cock. He dropped flat just as the gun spoke, the bullet driving into the tree trunk above him. He fired before the echoes of the first shot had died, aiming at the gun flash. He kept on until his gun was empty, throwing his bullets low and laying them a foot apart. He rolled and lay flat as he loaded his .45. A moment before, the night had been made hideous with gun thunder. Now there was only silence and the stink of burned powder.

The rest of Dagget's bunch was not around, or they would have opened up. Again panic took the bottom out of Clay's middle. They might have killed Vicky and the cook and gone on, leaving this man to burn the buildings.

He tried to wait, tried to remain motionless and silent while he listened for sounds of life from the man in front of the cookshack, but he could not. He had to know what was in the house. He bellied forward, pausing often to listen. There was no sound anywhere around the buildings. Then he moved again, and his outstretched hand fell upon a body.

He scratched a match across the cookshack wall and held it away from him. The tiny flame leaped up, was caught in the night wind, and died, but it let Clay see that the man was dead. He lay on his back, sightless black eyes staring upward, blood bubbling on his lips under a flaring yellow mustache.

Quickly Clay stepped into the cookshack and lighted the lamp. He lifted it from the table and held it high so that he could see into the corners of the room. The cook was sprawled at the end of the table, a bullet hole between his eyes. Then Clay saw a can of coal oil and a wad of paper on the floor. The story, then, was plain to read. Dagget had sent this man to burn Triangle S.

A lantern hung from a nail on the wall. Clay lighted it, blew out the lamp, and dragged the man he had shot inside. He shut the door, and made a quick search of the house, bunkhouse, and barns. No one else was around. He was tired and hungry, but he could not stop now. He mounted and rode south, the night solid blackness all around him. Sometime later the sky cleared, and stars made tiny winking dots. Still later a half moon rose over the Blue Mountains, and washed the flat with its chalk-white light.

Clay kept his roan at as fast a pace as he could; but the horse was tired, and the miles fell behind at a snaillike rate. He rode slack in the saddle, sometimes dozing, chin on his chest, and then he would come suddenly alive, aware of the desert smells, the touch of pine-scented wind on his cheeks, the distant call of a coyote. With all this there was always the terrible fear that he was too late, that Vicky Starr had gone on to Main's Flying M.

He crossed Crooked River and was in the junipers, a black sea stretching endlessly on both sides of the road. Before dawn he reached Lava City, put his horse away, and stumbled into the River Inn. Clutching the desk, he fought down the weariness that was trying to pull him into a bottomless pit. He asked thickly, "Vicky Starr here?"

The clerk stirred, rubbed his eyes, and rose from his chair to stand behind the desk. "I don't know that it's any of your—"

Temper, already raw in Clay Bond, beat at him like the rush of a searing wind. He grabbed the front of the clerk's shirt and shook him. "Damn you, I'm making it my business. Is she here?" He slammed him against the wall.

The clerk hit hard, lost his footing, and slid to the floor, head rapping against the wall. He ran the tip of his tongue over dry lips, and said, "Look, mister. I've got orders. You ain't bothering Miss Starr. Not tonight. Now go to hell."

"Is she here?"

"Yes, she's here, but if you try—"

Clay rubbed his face, trembling with relief. "All right, all right. Just give me a room."

He intended to get up early enough to catch Vicky at

breakfast; but the sleepless night and the long hours in the saddle had drained too much from him, and it was nearly noon when he woke. He dressed and asked at the desk for Vicky.

"Dunno where she is," the clerk said. "She waited here in the lobby for Jason Wade, and they left together."

Clay went into the dining-room and had dinner. He had slept like a dead man, his fears for Vicky's safety momentarily allayed. Now they returned to plague him. Evidently she had waited here in Lava City for Wade. According to Kyle, Wade had been told to send word to Vicky that Akin wanted to see her. Clay found it hard to believe that Jason Wade had any part in Main's murderous schemes, for he had instinctively liked the real estate man. Nor could he believe that George Akin was still alive.

By the time he had finished eating, the full weight of yesterday's worry was upon him. He paid for his meal and asked where he would find Wade's office.

"Just past the Red Crow saloon," the man said. "Says 'Lava City Townsite Company' on the window. You can't miss it."

"Thanks." Clay swung out of the hotel.

He half ran down the street, eyes searching both walks in the hope he'd see Vicky; but neither she nor Jason Wade was in sight. He passed the Red Crow, found Wade's office empty except for a thin-nosed woman who gave him a chill stare of disapproval, her eyes fixing on his gun.

"Is Wade in town?" Clay asked.

"No, but if you're interested in buying Lava City property—"

"I want to see Wade."

"He left for Saul Benton's place several hours ago."

"Was Vicky Starr with him?"

The woman hesitated, one long finger pressed against

the side of her thin nose. She said finally, "Yes, but it was merely a business trip, and there was nothing—"

Clay wheeled out of the office, not waiting to hear the rest of what she had to say. He ran down the boardwalk, rammed his way through a knot of settlers in front of the Red Crow, and raced on to the stable. Five minutes later he was riding eastward, some of the tension going out of him. Vicky would likely stay the night at Benton's. He would find her there.

He rode with the sun at his back, his shadow gradually lengthening before him. The pines dropped behind, junipers lined the road, and then he was atop the ridge where he had stopped after leaving Benton's. It was here that Vicky had caught him.

For long minutes Clay sat his saddle, staring at the black spot where his fire had been. He thought, *It's been only a few days, but it seems like a year.* Lifting his head, he looked out across the high desert, gray with sage or brown where its face was creased by long lines of rimrock, with here and there a lone juniper that made a small black dot in the distance. Again he felt the sweep of the empty miles, the pressure of the silence, and he thought of what it would be like with the sage and junipers cleared away, the sandy soil turned, and settlers' tar-paper shacks dotting the desert.

It was here that Vicky told him he was a little mixed up, that somebody else could straighten him out. He was straightened out, he told himself, and Vicky had done it. It was here, too, that she had said the railroad meant law and the end of Bronc Main's empire; and that was right. Main was the last of his kind. He would die before he gave up what he claimed as his, but other men might die at his hands before his end came.

Clay went on, and presently the sun was lost behind the Cascades, and darkness moved in swiftly. The roadhouse was a cluster of lights before him. He heard a hound dog bark, and Benton's shout, "Shut up your mouth, Nip." A chill touched his spine. It seemed to him he had lived this moment before. Then he remembered. It had been the same when he had ridden into Benton's yard a few nights before.

He reined up and swung down, staying away from the light patch in front of the house. Benton said, "I've got a bed for you, stranger, and some supper that ain't been et. Hell of a long ride from here to Burns."

Clay stood behind his horse, caution bringing his hand down to his gun and lifting it in leather. He dropped it so that it rode easily in the holster, his gaze swinging around the yard. Three horses were racked at the hitch pole. One was Vicky's. Relief was in him. He had been in time.

"I'll take that bed, Saul," Clay said. "Likewise some of your supper that ain't been et."

Clay watered his horse and loosened the cinch, watching Benton cross the yard to him. When the old man was close, he peered into Clay's face, swearing softly. "It's Bond. Damned if it ain't. You riding out of the country to stay this time?"

"No." Clay led his horse to the hitch pole. "I want to see Vicky."

Benton stood rooted there, breathing hard. Clay turned toward the house and reached the porch before he realized that the old man was not following. He swung back just as Benton started toward him in weaving steps. He called, his voice trembling, "Bond, don't go inside."

Clay sensed a fear in the old man that had brought him close to panic. He asked, "What's the matter with you, Saul? I'm hungry."

"Come on in," a man said from the doorway.

Again he dropped his right hand to gun butt. He made

a slow turn, sensing familiarity in the voice, but he was unable at the moment to identify the speaker. He moved quickly toward the porch. The man made a slender figure against the light, his face shadowed. As Clay climbed the steps, the other walked away from the door so that he melted into the darkness.

Clay said, "Thanks for the invitation. Benton didn't seem real hospitable."

"Funny gent, that Benton," the man said. "For years he bows and scrapes around in front of Bronc Main, but now that he's too old to fight, he gets hard. Throws in with a drifter named Clay Bond and tries to save his life. That's being a damned fool 'cause Bronc's got this Bond hombre tagged for killing."

Clay stood on the porch facing the man, the shaft of light between them. He still could not see the face, but he had placed the voice. It was Cash Taber, Bronc Main's foreman, the man Benton said knew guns better than cows. This, then, was Main's play. He had stationed Taber here to see that Clay did nothing to stop Vicky from going on into the desert after George Akin.

"Let's go inside, Taber. We'll finish this where the light's good."

Chapter Sixteen: DUEL BY LAMPLIGHT

FOR A MOMENT Cash Taber did not move. There was no sound from Saul Benton except his ragged breathing. It had been inevitable from the moment Clay Bond rode into Benton's yard that he would draw against Taber, and the gunman must have sensed it. He said at last, "I guess it would be better inside. Now, if it was Lew Dagget in your boots, he'd shoot as soon as I got in the light; but you're the kind of fool who's cursed with a conscience."

Benton called, "Vicky's in the house."

Taber moved into the front room that served as a parlor for the roadhouse, saying, "She's in her room. Keep her there, Wade."

Jason Wade was coming down the stairs. He saw at once what was going to happen, and stopped before he reached the bottom, eyes instinctively lifting to the hall above him.

Clay followed Taber, swinging away from him to stand against the east wall. The lamp was on a small table in front of him and to his right. Taber turned, thin lips pulled into a grin, sharp-featured face alive with his pleasure.

"You know, Bond, I kind of like you. I like any man who's got guts. Trouble is you ain't smart or you'd be on my side. Kyle allowed that's where you'd wind up; but it ain't so, or you wouldn't be here."

"That's right," Clay breathed.

Taber was playing cat-and-mouse with Clay, enjoying each moment of his dallying. He stood beside the tall walnut whatnot that was set against the west wall, long arms hanging motionless at his sides, grace and quickness and muscular co-ordination all part of him, physical characteristics that Clay had found in every gunman he had known. Too, there was another element in him, a pantherlike cruelty that made him like the grim trade he followed.

Deliberately Taber raised a hand to his shirt pocket, lifted tobacco and paper, and rolled a smoke. It was, Clay thought, a gesture of cold disdain aimed to tighten his enemy's nerves. He sealed the cigarette, slipped it into his mouth, and lighted it.

"What's the idea of bringing Vicky here?" Clay asked.

"She wants to see George Akin. Bronc invited her out to the Flying M to have a look."

"You're saying he's alive?"

"Sure he's alive." Taber shot an amused glance at Wade, still standing motionless on the stairs. "Tell him, Jason."

"I saw him," Wade said. "Taber took me out to Main's ranch. Akin was wounded, so he hasn't been able to leave the Flying M."

Clay didn't know whether Wade was lying or not, but he recognized the game. The gunman expected him to look up at Wade; then Taber meant to draw. But Clay did not lift his eyes to the promoter. Quick sharp steps sounded along the hall. Benton squalled, "Keep her up there, Wade."

"Make your play," Clay called.

For the first time he saw behind the cool mask that Taber wore, saw what prompted the little gestures he had made to prove his certainty of victory. The gunman harbored the same fears that any man had when his life hung in the balance. If that had not been true, he would not have resorted to the trick of trying to draw Clay's attention to Wade.

For a moment Taber hesitated, eyes pinned on Clay. Wade had bolted up the stairs. Vicky cried, "Don't let Taber—" Then the gunman made his draw.

He was smooth and fast, but not fast enough for the job he had given himself. His gun was still unfired when Clay's Colt roared. The first bullet took Taber high in the right shoulder. It turned him, before his hammer could drop, so that his slug went wild. Clay's second shot, thundering into the echoes of the first, caught him in the chest.

Clay paced forward, finger still tight on the trigger. As if from a great distance, he heard the shrill sound of Vicky's scream; he heard Benton's awed voice, "You got him, Bond."

The lamp flame had flickered uneasily when the guns spoke. Now it steadied. Smoke rose and spread across the ceiling like a gently moving veil, the smell of it an acrid stench. Gun sounds, held within the confines of the room, battered against the walls, were thrown back, and died. It was only seconds, but it seemed an hour that Taber swayed there beside the whatnot, his gun on the floor, right hand gripping the bloody front of his shirt.

Slowly Taber brought his eyes to Clay. There was no hate in them, no accusation, only the calm acceptance of his eventual destiny. "I told Bronc the night you got here that you was a tough hand. I said we'd better take—care—of—you." Then he went down, controls gone, and the room shook with his fall.

Benton rushed in, dropped to his knees, and picked up Taber's wrist. He rose and faced Clay, a scrawny hand coming up to wipe the sweat from his forehead. He said hoarsely, "You just wouldn't bluff, Bond. That was how you got him."

Clay nodded and holstered his gun. "Let's put him away. You can send him to town in the morning."

"I'll send him in now," Benton said. "I ain't keeping him around to haunt me tonight. Come on. We'll tote him out to the barn."

He called a man from the back of the house. Clay helped wrap Taber in a sheet, and they carried him outside to a wagon. Benton's man harnessed a team and hooked up. Benton had laid a canvas over the body and turned toward the house. He said, still awed by what had happened, "I pegged you for a dead man, Bond. I didn't give you no show at all against that gunslick." He took another deep breath. "I told you when you was here before that Bronc Main don't overlook nothing. You'd best be riding."

"I'm done riding." They had reached the house, and now Clay put out a hand to stop Benton. He asked softly, "What about Wade?"

"He's square," Benton answered quickly. "He ain't lying about seeing Akin, but what I want to know is how you're gonna keep Vicky from going out there."

"I don't know." Clay went on into the house.

"I'll tell Martha to get your grub on," Benton said, pushing past him.

For a time Clay paced around the parlor, smoking, restlessness in him. By killing Cash Taber he had settled nothing. It simply meant that Bronc Main had missed again. When a man once took the road to murder, there was no turning back. Neither Vicky nor Clay would be safe until Main was dead.

When the meal was ready he was not hungry; but he forced himself to eat. Then he leaned back and rolled a cigarette, and saw Jason Wade in the doorway looking at him.

"Where's Vicky?"

"In bed. We're leaving at sunup for the Flying M." Wade's eyes pushed at him. "Taber was our passport, Bond. You played hell killing him."

"He was your passport to Boot Hill," Clay flung back. "And if you'd been looking you'd have noticed I didn't have no choice about killing Taber."

"You could have ridden on," Wade said angrily. "We've had nothing but trouble since you came back."

"Trouble started a long time before that, friend." Clay rose. "Are you sure you saw Akin?"

"Sure I'm sure. I know him. Used to see him around Lava City."

"How did he happen to be at Flying M?"

"I told you he'd been wounded. Main took care of him."

"Did you talk to him?"

"Sure I talked to him. What are you getting at?"

"Did you talk to him alone?"

Wade chewed his lower lip, frowning. "No. Taber was always with me, but that didn't make any difference. Akin was in bed and he was conscious. Outside of being thin, he looked pretty well."

"What was his story?"

"He was riding back and forth across the desert, figuring out the best route for the railroad, when somebody shot him. He doesn't know who. When he came around, he was at the Flying M."

Clay walked around the table, thinking of this. Bronc Main playing the Good Samaritan made no sense at all. He turned and gave Wade a long studying stare. The promoter was fingering an elk-tooth charm that dangled from his watch chain, making no effort to hide his resentment.

"Are you sure Akin was telling the yarn he wanted to?" Clay demanded.

"Just Taber and me in Akin's bedroom. Taber wasn't holding a gun on him, if that's what you're driving at."

"Main wasn't around?"

Wade shook his head. "He's in Prineville. Taber didn't know when he was coming back." He tapped the table nervously. "I don't see what's worrying you, Bond. There's nothing wrong now. The whole trouble was that Main didn't want Akin running around over the desert because he thought the Oregon Southern would give up building when Akin disappeared; but Paddon showed up. Now Main sees he's licked, so he's going to let Akin travel as soon as he's able. Right now Akin wants to see Vicky, and Main says for her to come out to the Flying M."

"Main ain't licked, which same you ought to know," Clay said hotly. "What kind of a man would call himself King of the Desert?"

"A gent who's too big for his pants," Wade admitted. "But what's he up to, telling Vicky she can see Akin?"

"If you wasn't blind you'd see what he was up to. The trouble with you is that you want to believe he's on the level. Now you keep Vicky here. I'm going to the Flying M in the morning."

"It's my job, Clay," Vicky said from the doorway.

She was wearing a maroon robe, the cord knotted in front of her, her long black hair down her back. Clay had never seen her so pretty, he thought, or so unattainable.

He said, "It's a job I'm a little better qualified for than you are."

"I don't think so. You'll be killed if you show up at the Flying M, but Main will know that neither Jason nor I will pull a gun on him."

"Main won't be sure of that." Clay told her what had happened at Triangle S.

She dropped into a chair, color leaving her face. She whispered, "Why would they kill Cooky?"

"Main's kill-crazy. When a man gets that way, he don't need a reason. Where were your men?"

"Up Pigeon Creek." She looked down at the floor, fighting for self-control. Then she said in a low tone, "Cooky was one of the best friends I had. I've known him ever since I was a girl. He used to cook in a hotel in Prineville until Dad died and I hired him." She looked up, her lips quivering. "What do they want, Clay?"

"You and me, I reckon. Paddon says that if Kyle could get his hands on the right-of-way agreements we signed, and then we disappeared, the Oregon Southern would be tied up for a long time."

She nodded, her emotions controlled. "But Kyle won't get his hands on the right-of-way agreements. They're licked, Clay. Akin is a big man in the company. The minute he gets on his feet, he'll build the road."

Clay nodded. "That makes him Main's ace in the hole. Once the desert swallows you and Akin and Wade, there's nobody left but Paddon who gives a damn about the railroad."

"What can you do by going out to the Flying M?" Vicky demanded.

He could have told her his love for her was enough to make him risk his life to save hers, but he didn't. She probably would not believe him, so he only said, "Depends on what I find."

"I was wrong before when I tried to find Akin," she said tonelessly. "I'm sure now that Main would have treated me the same as he would a man; but this time it's different. Taber told me that Main is afraid he'll be in trouble if he keeps Akin any longer; so he's trying to satisfy Akin's whims. He can't travel yet, but there's something he wants to tell me personally. That's why Main told Taber to take me to the Flying M."

"You don't believe that yarn?" Clay asked incredulously.

"I admit it's a small straw, but I've got to reach for it. You see, George Akin means to me what my father should have meant. He stayed at Triangle S when he first came to the Deschutes, and I talked to him a lot." She made a small gesture as if begging Clay to believe this. "I guess you'd say he gave me a way to live."

She said it honestly. Clay did not understand, for according to his way of thinking a person found his own way to live and no one else could give it to him. But Sid Starr had not been his father. He sensed then for the first time how much George Akin meant to her. He said, as if agreeing to the necessity of her going, "I guess we have to play it the way we see it."

"That's right, Clay."

Vicky rose and moved to the door, then stopped to look back at him, her full lips softly pressed. She turned and went up the stairs. When he heard her door close, he nodded to Wade. "You might as well go to bed. I guess I didn't get anywhere with Vicky."

"Ain't you gonna make her stay here, Bond?" Benton

demanded.

"Did you ever see anybody make Vicky stay some place where she didn't want to stay?" Clay asked.

"Well, no."

"More sense around here than I thought there'd be," Wade grunted. "You're dreaming up a nightmare, Bond. I've had some dealings with Main, and I've always found him on the level."

Clay yawned. "Go to bed."

Wade left the dining-room and climbed the stairs to his room.

Benton had been watching Clay. Now he said hotly, "Damn you, Bond, if you don't do something, I will. I'll steal their horses. I'll lock 'em in their rooms. I ain't letting Vicky go out there just because she thinks she owes so much to George Akin. All the railroads in the world ain't worth her little finger."

"You're right, my friend." Clay rolled a smoke, his eyes on the brown paper. "King of the Desert. Funny thing, Benton, how big a man gets in his own mind."

"Well, are you going to do anything?"

"Yeah, figured I would. Where is the Flying M?"

"'Bout twenty miles east of here. Maybe less. Then you turn north and go another three, four miles. This side of Hampton Buttes."

"I'll find it." Clay moved into the parlor and sat down on the leather couch. "You sleep good?"

"Not lately."

"Wake me at midnight. I'll pull out then. And you keep 'em here in the morning."

Benton scratched the back of his long neck, worried eyes on Clay. "You know what'll happen to you if Main's there?"

"I'm gambling he won't be there." Clay yawned. "Now blow that lamp out. I aim to sleep."

Chapter Seventeen: DEAD MAN ALIVE

DAWN FOUND CLAY at the junction of the road and the wheel ruts that twisted northward to the Flying M. Never one to fool himself about realities, he knew he had no chance at all unless he got to the ranch before Main returned from Prineville. Probably Dagget would need a doctor for his arm. What happened after that would depend on whether Main chose to strike at Paddon or to return to the Flying M to see whether Vicky had taken the bait. It was his guess that Main would come to the ranch.

He rode north, stopping often to listen. There was only a singing silence upon a half-lighted world, this period between darkness and day when the desert night life had retired to sanctuaries and day life had not yet awakened. Then morning showed above the eastern rimrock, and the bulge of the sun along the horizon was a red arc. To his left the buttes and rocky rims were scarlet; to his right purple shadows hung like evanescent mist. Then he reached a ridge and looked down upon the Flying M buildings, and it was full daylight.

Still Clay rode with caution, for he had no way of knowing whether Main and Dagget were here. The ranch house was a squat, ugly structure, entirely without paint, its square lines unrelieved even by a porch. Beyond was the usual cluster of barns and sheds and corrals, all stained dull gray by years of weathering. There was nothing green about the place; drab desert was all around.

A column of smoke lifted from the chimney of the house. There were horses in the corrals, a fact which proved nothing. If Akin was being held prisoner, Main would have left a few men here. Or, if there was only a man or two, Main would probably want fresh horses on hand ready to saddle.

Clay racked his roan and walked around the house, his gun riding loosely in leather. He had this one bad moment before he knocked on the back door. If it broke, it would come fast with bullets blasting life from him without warning, for Bronc Main would take no chances from here on.

The door squeaked open. A bearded man stared at Clay with his one good blue eye. The other, a glass one, was brown and seemed to be looking at some distant point beyond the barn. The man said, "Howdy, mister," and wiped his doughy hands on a flour-sack apron.

"Howdy," Clay said. "Main around?"

"Ain't you calling a mite early?"

Clay grinned. "Maybe. I've been riding a good part of the night. I wanted to catch Main before some of that Oregon Southern outfit rode in. I aim to make him an offer for all the beef he's got to sell."

"You belong to Kyle's Columbia & Cascade outfit?"

"That's right. Kyle says we're building for sure, but we ain't figgering on running no line across the desert. Anyhow, Kyle allows he'll have five, six thousand men in the canyon afore snow flies."

"Take a lot of beef to feed that many men." The one-eyed man stepped back. "Come in, stranger. Bronc ain't here right now, but he'll be along. Et breakfast?"

Clay shook his head. "I could stand some."

"Nobody here now but me and Mullins and an old coot named Akin. The rest of the outfit will be here tonight. Mebbe sooner. Then I'll be cooking from hell to breakfast. You don't need to worry about Bronc selling the Oregon Southern any beef. He wouldn't sell them a stink if he had a skunk to make it." The cook plodded over to the stove and dropped some juniper into the firebox. He set the lid back and made a slow turn. "What did you say your name was?"

"Didn't say." Clay saw the man's forehead pucker as if a new thought was working in his mind. "It's Jones. You don't figger Main will be here afore evening?"

"Might be here anytime." The cook moved past the long table and, opening a door, called, "Breakfast. Git in here, Mullins, afore I throw it out."

The man who walked through the door first seemed very old, his gray skin drawn tightly across a bony face. He walked slowly as if there was little strength left in him. His dark eyes swung to Clay and turned away as if he saw him as nothing more than another gunman. He would, Clay guessed, be George Akin. Another man was behind him, bull-necked and redheaded, with tiny green eyes that bored into Clay's.

"Who's this hombre?" the red-haired one asked.

The cook had moved back to the stove. He picked up a chunk of juniper, balanced it in his hand, puzzled eyes on Clay. "Says his handle's Jones. Works for Kyle and wants to buy beef. Says he wants to see Bronc."

"That's right," Clay said. "Rode all night. I'm hungry enough to eat—"

"He rode all night, Mullins," the cook cut in. "Get that? He rode all night so he could get here ahead of some Oregon Southern man."

Mullins said, "So," as if he considered Clay's story credible.

"Well, don't stand there doing nuthin'," the cook bawled. "Bronc hired you to fight. Not me."

A gunshot could be heard a long way across the desert. It might bring Bronc Main on the run. Clay moved toward the redhead. "What's biting Cooky? All I want is breakfast and a bed to sleep in till Main shows up."

Mullins blinked, looked from Clay to the cook and back to Clay. "Dunno what's biting him, mister. Where's that breakfast, Squint?"

The cook took a long breath. "Mullins, you ain't bright enough to draw fighting wages. This hombre ain't Kyle's man. If he was, he'd know damned well Main wouldn't sell no beef to the Oregon Southern, and he wouldn't be giving us no cock-and-bull yarn 'bout riding all night to get here ahead of—"

Mullins grabbed for his gun. Clay hit him, shoved him against the table, and ducked just as the cook let go with the stick of juniper. It slammed into the wall and crashed to the floor. Mullins swung a wild fist at Clay's face and missed and took a right on his chin. Dazed and rammed against the table, he could do nothing but paw futiley at Clay.

Akin was no help. He stared blankly at the fight as if it held no interest for him. The cook picked up another piece of wood and ran at Clay, yelling, "I'll bat your head down between your ears, you damned spy." Clay wheeled, drove a foot into the cook's belly and knocked him flat on the floor. Mullins bounced back from the table and tried again for his gun. Then his hand dropped away and he began to curse, for he was staring into the muzzle of Clay's Colt.

"You're smart, Cooky," Clay said. "I figgered Oregon Southern's dinero would be as good as anybody's."

The cook sucked in his breath. "Not on Flying M it ain't. What are you here for?"

"Akin." Clay nodded at the old man. "Where can we lock up these buzzards?"

Akin was on his feet, clawlike fingers gripping the edge of the table. "Who are you?"

"Clay Bond. I'm Vicky's friend."

Then George Akin came alive. Color swept into his face; he was breathing in short excited pants. "Clay Bond. You own the place on the river. Vicky." He came around the table and leaned on it. "You're going to get me out of here. You are, aren't you, Bond?" He was pathetic in his eagerness.

"That's right," Clay told him. "Is there some place we can put these hombres?"

"There's a storeroom back there." He pointed a trembling hand at a door beyond the pantry. "I think it will hold them."

Clay motioned to the door. "Pull off your gun belt, Mullins. Lay it on the table."

Cursing, Mullins obeyed. The cook got to his feet, one hand holding his stomach, his good eye frosty with hate. "Bronc'll get you. Bronc'll get you as sure as hell will scorch your feathers, you damned rooster."

They tramped through the door and into the storeroom. Clay took a quick look inside, saw that the walls were solid and that there was nothing here but a few barrels of flour, some sacks of sugar, and three hams hanging from the ceiling. He shut the door and twisted the big turnpin. When he swung around, Akin was at the oven piling his plate high with biscuits.

"We'd better travel," Clay said. "Main might—"

"I'm going to eat," Akin muttered. "I'm going to fill my stomach. They've been starving me, but now I'm going to eat till I burst. Come and have some breakfast."

They shouldn't take the time, but Clay doubted if Akin could ride until he had eaten. Food might give him enough strength to make a few miles at least. He poured coffee and forked bacon from the frying-pan onto a platter. He asked, "Can you ride if you get some grub inside you?"

"I'll have to. I won't wait for Main. They shot me and then kept me half starved so I couldn't get away if I had a chance." He gulped a biscuit and, lifting his eyes to Clay, asked, "Did Paddon get to the Deschutes?"

Only then did Clay realize that Akin knew nothing of what had been happening on the river. "He's there, all right." While Akin ate he told him what had happened.

"It's Vicky's work," Akin murmured when Clay finished. "She's a wonderful girl."

"She is that. Last night at Benton's she told me you meant to her what her father should have. She said you gave her a way of life."

Akin put down his coffee cup. "I did everything I could for her. I owed her that. She took me in when she didn't know why I had come to central Oregon. Fed me and gave me a bed. She thought I was just fishing. After I told her why I was there, she began to talk. Little pieces at a time. Told me about her father and how she hated everything he had done. I guess I told her about myself, what I believed in and what I'd done." He turned his coffee cup between his fingers, face thoughtfully sober. "We all have a certain standard—a code, I guess you'd call it. Vicky's picked a mighty good one to live by."

Clay rose and, taking the coffeepot from the stove, filled their cups. "Looks to me like Main aimed to get her out of here and kill both of you."

"That's right," Akin said somberly. "I didn't know until after Wade was here. Then Mullins told me." He gestured wearily. "I couldn't have told Wade anything even if I had known what Main meant to do. Mullins was standing in the next room with a gun in his hand. Wade didn't see it, but there was a knothole in the wall just opposite my head." He clenched a bony hand and pounded the table. "But I would have told Wade if I had known. It would have been better if they'd killed both me and Wade than to have let him fetch Vicky out here to be murdered."

Clay finished his coffee. "If you're able to fork a horse, we'd better ride."

"I'll stay on if you have to tie me—" Akin stopped, the unmistakable sound of horses coming to them. He slumped forward, a trembling hand upsetting his cup. He grabbed at it and set it upright, the coffee flowing across the table top. "It's too late," he whispered. "That's Main now."

Chapter Eighteen: TRAPPED

CLAY WHEELED FROM THE TABLE to look out through the back door. Main was riding in at the head of his men. Dagget, left arm in a sling, rode directly behind him. For a moment Clay stood paralyzed. The way the cook had talked, he had a feeling that Main was not expected back until later in the day. If he had had two hours, or even one, he could have got Akin away from the ranch house and into the desert. With any kind of luck they could have hidden out until dark and then gone on to Benton's roadhouse.

He had always held to the notion that a man made his own luck; but the hour of Bronc Main's return was one of those imponderables over which he had no control. It was sheer bad luck, and in this short moment as he stood staring at the Flying M riders, it seemed to him that he had no chance at all. He could bluff, and he could die with a gun in his hand, a sorry end for a man who, within a matter of days, finds within his reach the big things of life that he has long wanted.

At such a time a man's thoughts run with the tumbling rush of a clear mountain stream. Clay thought of his place on the river, the money Walt Paddon had given him for the right of way, the job and the big wages Paddon had promised. He thought of his future now that he had enough money to buy good stock, he thought of Vicky Starr, with whom he wanted to share his future. He did not know what lay between them; but, whatever it was, he felt confident he could surmount it, given time and life. His only regret now was that he had not told her he loved her.

He turned back to the table, picked up Mullins's gun, and gave it to Akin. He said, "We'll fight. I'm going out to meet Main. You stay inside."

"It's suicide—" Akin began.

"Sure, and it's suicide if we let 'em drill us like ducks on a pond. Watch the door into the storeroom. Your job is to keep Mullins and the cook off my back in case they bust that door open."

Drawing gun, Clay swung to the door, knowing that there was no chance at all if Main's crew scattered, or if Akin allowed the men in the storeroom to break out. It would have been a fair gamble if he had a strong man in Akin's place; but Akin had been wounded and half starved, and the great courage that must have been in him once had drained away. However, there was no choice. He had to depend upon Akin, for he could not watch both the men in front of him and the storeroom door.

Main and his men were dismounting as Clay stepped out of the house. He heard Main bawl, "Get them saddles on fresh horses. Won't take Squint long to get breakfast."

"Take a look, Bronc," Dagget shouted, jabbing a forefinger at Clay's roan. "Where'd that animal come from? It ain't Mullins's horse."

Main gave out a startled whistle. "Looks like we caught ourselves a rabbit. That's Bond's horse, ain't it?"

"That's right," Clay called, "only you've caught a rabbit that's got teeth. I'll plug the first man who makes a wrong move, and I'm hoping it'll be you, Main."

Only then was Main aware that Clay had come out of the house. The cowman made a slow ponderous turn. There was no humor on his big face, no hint of a smile on his meaty lips. He stood like a great rock, thick legs

spread, as arrogant as he had been the night he was hunting Vicky at Benton's roadhouse; but Clay sensed that his
arrogance was more sham than real. The other time Cash
Taber had been with him. Now there was no Cash Taber
to lean upon, and Dagget and the others would wait for
him to make the first move. When he did, he would be a
dead man; so he played for time, seeking a way by which
he could safely maneuver out of this situation.

Without turning his massive body to look at Dagget,
Main said, "Lew, we've got a rabbit to skin."

Dagget backed away from Main. "This is a job for
Taber, Bronc. Don't count me in."

Clay laughed, a contemptuous laugh that brought a
dull red into Dagget's battered face. "You've got a tough
hand in Dagget, Main. He's right down ornery when he
can swing on a man who can't swing back."

"You won't do no more swinging," Dagget shouted
hoarsely. "Wait till Taber meets up with you. He's been
wanting to notch his sights on you."

"It'll be quite a wait. Taber tried last night, but his
luck was sure bad. Main, I've got Mullins and your cook
locked up in the house. Akin's got a gun, and after what
you've done to him he'll enjoy plugging you."

"You've got us hipped," Main admitted, ignoring the
news of Taber's death, "but you've bitten off quite a chew.
What do you figger you'll do with us?"

"Drop your gun belts, and I'll throw you in with Mullins and your cook. All me and Akin want right now is a
chance to get out of here."

"That won't settle nothing."

"We'll settle after I get Akin to Lava City. Now drop
your gun belts."

"Don't do it, boys," Main said with more coolness than
Clay expected. "Go ahead and drill me, Bond, but I ain't
drawing on you while you stand there holding a gun on

me. I'm pretty damned sure you won't plug a man who don't have an iron in his hand."

Dagget had moved away to stand against the corral. The rest had fanned out behind Main and stood waiting. Dangerous men, but not so dangerous as if Cash Taber had been with them. The kind of leadership that the gunman would have given them was missing. Still, some unexpected thing might start the shooting. If it did, Clay's slim chance of pulling this off was gone.

The seconds ribboned out, no one moving, and Clay called impatiently, "I ain't gonna stand here all day. Drop your gun belts."

Still none of them moved to obey, and Main gave out a short taunting laugh. "You've been a fool for luck, Bond, but a man don't go on riding high forever. You're forgetting one thing. I'm king out here, and I aim to stay king."

Clay stepped away from the house. Time was running out. He heard Mullins and the cook banging on the storeroom door. He wasn't sure whether the turnpin would hold; he didn't know where Akin was or what he was doing, and he could not look back to see.

"Come on, come on," he said. "I'll give you about ten more seconds."

"We'll wait it out," Main said coolly. "I've got your size, Bond. You just ain't big enough to run this desert, and your friend Paddon ain't big enough to build a railroad out here. I told you I'd teach you some manners. We'll start with this business of you holding a gun on a bunch of men. That's bad manners. Awful bad." He started forward, dust spurting under each downward stroke of his boots.

Clay said, "That's far enough, Main. I've got a question to ask before you come any farther. Are you ready to die?"

The Flying M owner stopped, puzzled. "Now what kind of a damn fool question is that?"

"It's the biggest question you'll ever have to answer. Start thinking on it because, if you keep coming, I'll drop you whether you've got a gun in your hand or not."

Main stood perfectly still, head slanted forward, lips twitching under his mustache. Like all men of his kind, he had never considered his eventual defeat, that some day the same violent death he had decreed for others would be his. He had thought he had put his finger on Clay's weakness, but now he wasn't sure.

"You ain't tough enough to pull that trigger, Bond. That's why I'm going on being King of the Desert."

"You make a mistake now, and it'll be your last one," Clay warned. "The way I've got it figgered out, the Almighty won't hold it against me if I burn you down."

"Come on, boys." Main made a sweeping gesture toward his men. "He won't shoot."

Again he started across the dusty yard, black eyes held on Clay as unwaveringly as twin shotgun muzzles. It took more cold courage than Clay had thought the big cowman possessed; but men's nerves can stand only so much, and this had come to the breaking-point. It was not what Clay wanted. Killing Bronc Main would not save his life and Akin's, and so he made one more desperate try.

"You're wrong, Main," Clay said evenly. "One more step. That's the last you'll take if you—"

He heard the storeroom door slam open, heard Mullins's and the cook's running steps across the kitchen. There was a shot. Clay started to turn and knew he could not; he saw triumph break across Main's face.

He fired, the dismal knowledge in him that he had failed. His bullet missed, for Main had thrown himself flat on the ground, and he had no second chance. Something struck him on the back of the head and knocked him flat on his face, and the sunlight was blotted out.

"Got him," the cook crowed. "Damn him, lock me up

in the storeroom, will he?"

Dagget was running forward, very brave now, his gun in his hand. "I'll kill him," he bawled. "He won't never—"

Main scrambled up, grabbed Dagget by his right arm and threw him down. "You're tough, Lew, now, ain't you? A minute ago you said this was Taber's job, but when Bond gets flat on his back you want to kill him."

Dagget rolled over and wiped dust from his face, whimpering in pain because he had fallen on his injured arm. Then he cried, "What the hell? You ain't gonna keep him alive?"

"You bet I'll keep him alive, leastwise till I figure out a way to beef him that won't look like murder. You ain't got a brain in your head, Lew." Main tapped his forehead. "If I wasn't smarter'n you are, I'd never have got where I am." He motioned to Mullins. "Take Bond and Akin upstairs and lock 'em up. You stay outside in the hall. Brady, put Bond's horse away. If the sheriff shows up, I'll do the talking—all of it."

Chapter Nineteen: DESERT RIDE

VICKY WOKE with the first of the morning sunlight falling across her bed. For a time she lay motionless, staring at the ceiling. She should get up. There was another long ride to make. She should get up now. Not in half an hour. Or five minutes. Now! But she didn't. She was tired, tired clear to the marrow of her bones. It seemed to her she had just spent an eternity in the saddle.

She wondered if anything in life was worth the price that a person must pay. Her father, for all the unflagging energy that drove him, had died an unhappy man. Not that he had ever spoken of it, but it was something she had sensed in him. Bronc Main, too, would be paying a price; and in the end he would pay more, although the idea had probably never occurred to him.

She thought of the goal she had set for herself, of balancing the evil her father had done by the good she could do. That was why she had plunged into this fight for a railroad. Now she considered the trouble and death it had brought; and the trouble was not yet finished. But it had brought Clay into her life, and she was glad of that, even though the door had somehow been shut between them.

Suddenly she threw the blanket back and jumped up. Clay might take it into his head to go on out to the Flying M. She opened the door and listened. Saul Benton and Jason Wade were talking, the housekeeper Martha rattling dishes in the dining-room; but she did not hear Clay's voice.

She dressed quickly and pinned up her hair. She was responsible for George Akin coming here to the Deschutes, and felt a responsibility for what had happened to him. That weight upon her conscience had driven her into the high desert to find Akin; it had brought her here again when Jason Wade sent the note. Because it was her job, she did not want Clay to do it for her.

Benton and Wade had already gone into the dining-room for breakfast when Vicky came down the stairs. She stood in the doorway, seeing that only the two were at the table, and she guessed the truth before she asked, "Where's Clay?"

"Gone," Benton said.

She came in and sat down at the table. "Where?"

Benton scratched the back of his neck and cleared his throat, eyes swinging to Wade and returning to Vicky's taut face. "He rode out to the Flying M, and he wants you to stay here where you'll be safe."

"Saul, have I ever stayed any place just because it was safe?"

"No, but—" Benton swallowed, then he shouted, "Hod

dang it, Vicky, this is different. You ought to know it after what Main did that evening Bond rode in. I don't mind saying I'm scared. It's time you was learning what it means to be scared, too."

"Don't you think Clay's scared?"

"Naw. He don't know what the word means."

"Then it's time he was finding out. And you're forgetting, Saul, that this time Main sent Taber to take me out there."

"And what do you figure it'll do to his disposition when he hears that Taber's dead?"

"I know what it'll do," she said calmly. "That's why I wanted to go instead of Clay. I didn't kill Taber. Clay did."

Benton cackled. "I'd sure like to be a mouse behind the door when Main hears about it. I figure it'll be the end of Mr. Bronc Main. If I didn't think that, I'd be making tracks out o' here." He motioned to her plate. "Eat your breakfast, and forget this business of going to the Flying M. It's in pretty good hands."

Wade had been eating, his eyes on his plate. Vicky threw him a glance, wondering. He had been so confident that there was no danger for them at the Flying M. Now he had the appearance of a thoroughly frightened man. He belonged in Lava City selling lots; he was out of place here, and he showed that he knew it.

Vicky said nothing more until the meal was finished. Then she rose, asking, "When did Clay leave?"

"Midnight."

"Then he'll be there by now. Come on, Jason."

Benton jumped up, kicking back his chair. "You ain't going out there. So help me Hannah, Clay said to keep you here, and I aim to do it if I have to hog-tie you and Wade. Clay'll be back by dark, and I'll gamble he'll have Akin with him."

"Then we'll meet him. Come on, Jason."

"Sit where you are, Wade." Benton moved toward Vicky, the corners of his thin-lipped mouth working. "Vicky, you can't do it. Give Clay a chance. Let him play his hand out."

"And let him die." She shook her head. "I'd never forgive myself for that. You see, Saul, there's one thing you don't understand. I'd rather die today knowing I'd done the best I could than live to be a hundred and know I had been a coward."

Benton sat down, his head bowed, and his voice was so low that she could hardly hear him. "I know, Vicky. I know better than you think I do. The only reason I've stuck here so long is because I didn't buck Main. I know enough to hang that ornery son, but I kept my mug shut because I knew what would happen to me if I talked. I'd have been happier to have died the day I was born."

"Saul, Saul, you're talking crazy." She laid a hand on his arm. "I brought you trouble when I came, but you didn't tell Main I was here. In my book, that makes you a brave man."

"Brave?" He laughed shakily. "I was ashamed of myself watching you and Clay. It done me a lot of good listening to that boy stand up to Bronc Main. I learned something I should have knowed all the time. Main ain't as big as he lets on."

"Then Jason and I won't have any trouble."

Wade rose, the charm that had been a part of him in Lava City now entirely gone. "I don't think I'll go, Vicky. I'm not used to riding, and I've done so much the last day or so that I can't look a horse in the face."

"Then don't look at the end that has the face," she said contemptuously. "In case you've forgotten, I'll remind you that it was your note that brought me to Lava City."

"But I didn't know Bond was going to shoot Taber," he

burst out. "Taber promised us safe conduct, but we don't know what we'll have now that he's dead."

"You know, Jason," Vicky said, "a lot of folks who have bought property in Lava City would like to see you now. You'd be real proud to have them see you, wouldn't you?"

"That's got nothing to do with this," he said rebelliously. "I'm just trying to develop a townsite."

"And you've promised your customers a railroad, but you don't want to run the risks it takes to bring it here. Akin risked his life. I'm willing to risk mine. And look at what Clay's doing."

"Clay's in love with you," Wade blurted. "I'm not. I'm not in love with George Akin, either. He knew what his chances were when he headed into the desert."

She stared at him, her back very straight, her blue-black eyes dark with loathing. Suddenly she turned and walked out. Benton got up and struck him across the face. "Get out there, you yellow son. If you don't go all the way with her and I ever see you again, I'll blow you apart."

Wade went, saying nothing, his face scarlet. He caught up with Vicky before she reached the corrals. They threw gear on their horses and mounted, and when they rode past the house Saul Benton was standing in front, a hand raised in farewell. Vicky smiled and waved, and they went on, riding eastward.

It was a silent ride, and it suited Vicky that way. She could not forget Wade's words, *Clay's in love with you.* How did Jason Wade know? Several times she glanced at his rigid face, but she could not bring herself to ask him. It must, she thought, be evident to everyone but her. How? She kept asking herself that.

Wade could not have heard Clay say it in words. Clay wouldn't. Not before he said it to her. She had to believe that, for it was not a thing to be talked about before everyone. It must be in the way he looked at her, the way he talked, the things he did. That was it, of course. *The things he did.* It was what had brought him to Benton's road-house; it was what had sent him on to the Flying M at midnight. Now she was following him when he had want-ed her to stay at Benton's.

For the first time since she had left the roadhouse the thought that this was wrong came into her mind. Benton might have been right. Maybe she was spoiling what Clay was doing. She pondered this long after they had made the turn from the Burns road toward the Flying M. When they came within sight of the buildings, she still had not made up her mind.

Suddenly Wade burst out, "We didn't have anything to do with Taber's killing. Remember that."

"We had everything to do with it," she said; "but that's something you wouldn't understand. Have you got a gun?"

He said, "No."

They rode down the long slope. There were horses in the corrals, and a number of men were idling in the yard; but Clay was not among them, and his roan was not in sight. As she and Wade came closer, the feeling that some-thing was terribly wrong grew in her. If Main and his riders had returned while Clay was here, he could not have escaped with Akin. By this time he was either dead, or a prisoner.

They reined up in front of the house. None of the Fly-ing M hands moved or called out. For a moment Vicky sat her saddle, staring at them and hating them as she wondered if one of these men had killed her cook. Then the front door slammed open, and Bronc Main strode out of the house, grinning broadly as if he expected them and was pleased that they had come.

"Light and rest your saddles," Main called. "Time for dinner."

No, Vicky thought, this wasn't right. She dismounted

and tied, and as Wade moved past her she whispered,
"When a mean dog tries to lick your hand, Jason, it's time
to look out."

Chapter Twenty: PRISONERS

IT WAS STILL MORNING when Clay regained consciousness.
He was on a bed, the sunlight that fell through an east
window throwing a long scarlet rectangle across the room.
He moved, slapping at the blinding light. For a time he
lay still, feeling the steady beat of pain across his temples.
Then he remembered what had happened, and sat up. He
fell back at once, for the instant he came upright, each
hammering beat felt as if someone was hitting him across
the head with a club.

"No hurry, son," George Akin said. "No hurry at all.
We'll be here a long time unless Main decides to kill us."

Clay turned, caught the sunlight full in his eyes, and
drew back against the wall. He sensed that Akin was sitting in a chair along the south wall, but it was a moment
before his vision cleared and he could actually see the
railroad man. He still seemed very old and thin, and his
shoulders were slack with weariness, but his eyes were
alive with a smoldering fire that Clay had not seen in them
before.

"Didn't know I had company," Clay said.

"I'm not much company," Akin said bitterly. "I hate
myself right now about as much as I hate Main and Mullins. I didn't do my job. If I had, you might have pulled
it off."

"What happened?"

"You'll remember I had Mullins's gun and you told me
to watch the storeroom door. I didn't. That's all. I just
didn't. I thought that door was too strong to bust open,
and I knew there were too many men in the yard for you

to handle if the shooting started. Main was coming at you, so I was looking at him when Mullins and Squint got out of the storeroom."

"I thought I heard a shot," Clay said.

Akin gestured wearily. "You did. I let go at Mullins and missed. I used to be able to shoot straight, but I've been kind of trembly lately. I guess I was excited, knowing how much depended on me. Anyhow, I didn't have another chance. Squint picked up a chunk of stovewood and threw it at you and Mullins hit me in the face. He knocked me down and kicked the gun across the room. I was groggy for a while, but I had sense enough to know you were out cold. Then I heard Main tell them to take you and me upstairs."

Clay rubbed the back of his head where the piece of wood had hit him. "Squint must be pretty handy with his stovewood."

"He's handy, all right, and he's mean. Doesn't take much to set his temper loose."

Clay rolled to the side of the bed and sat up, lips tightening against the pulsing beat of pain. Presently it eased. Akin, watching him, said, "I don't see why you punish yourself."

"Hell, if I don't get up, I won't be worth a damn."

"We're not going anywhere." Akin jabbed a thumb at the door. "Mullins is outside. I've got pretty well acquainted with that redhead, Bond. He'll shoot us both if we give him an excuse."

"Maybe not. Something funny about this. Why didn't Main beef us when it would have been easy?"

Akin rubbed his chin, eyes thoughtful. "Dagget wanted to kill you, and Main wouldn't let him. He's smart enough, Bond, if you want to call a man with his animal intelligence smart. He said something about beefing you so it wouldn't look like murder. I was too groggy to get it straight when the talk was going on, but I got the notion he thought the sheriff might show up."

Clay sat thinking about that, but it made little sense to him. He wondered if Akin had been out of his head and had dreamed the talk about the sheriff. Everything which Clay had heard since he'd come back indicated that Bronc Main was exactly what he claimed to be—King of the Desert. Still, there was only so much a sheriff could ignore. It was possible, too, that the lawman had been waiting for a definite charge against Main.

"Well, then," Clay said, "if that's the way it is, we've got till dark and no more. Main might be afraid the sheriff's watching the house." He gave Akin a thin grin. "We're in a tight, friend. Looks like I didn't do nothing but bring this to a boil."

"You did all you could. Anyhow, it's better than having Vicky ride out here."

Clay rose and walked to the south window. He put his hands against the casing to steady himself, for the slightest exertion brought the hammering back to his head and started the room spinning; but he held himself there until the dizziness left him. Whatever small chance of escape that he and Akin had was limited by time. It would take a clear head, and he wouldn't have one if he didn't start moving around.

Again Akin said, "I don't see why you punish yourself."

"We're getting out of here."

Akin shook his head. "I've been here for weeks, Bond. I just never had a chance to get out."

Clay stared down into the yard, saying nothing. He didn't want to hurt the old man's pride, but if he had been in Akin's place he would have been out of here before now. He saw at once it would be foolish to make a try through this window. Most of Main's crew were hunkered in the shade beside the barn. Even if he knotted the blankets together and swung down, he'd stop a bullet before he hit the ground. There might be a chance before dark if there was still time, but he doubted that there would be.

He turned to the east window and raised it. No one was in sight. He leaned out. Then a door opened, and Mullins said, "Wake up, did you, Bond?"

Clay pulled his head in and turned. Mullins was holding a gun, green eyes mocking him.

"Yeah, I woke up. I was just thinking I'd take a walk."

"Put the window down," Mullins ordered. "You'll do your walking right here."

Clay obeyed, saying, "Sure, I never argue with a man when he's holding a gun on me."

"That's sense, mister. You know, I ain't real happy about the way you hammered me around this morning."

Mullins stepped back into the hall and shut the door. Akin said, "See how it is?"

Clay rolled a smoke and fired it. He walked around the room, the hammering in his head subsiding. "I see, all right, but I ain't convinced."

"I was," Akin said bitterly. "I've been railroading for years, and I never built a road when there wasn't someone who wanted to stop me; but this is the worst I ever ran into. We aren't dealing with an ordinary man, Bond. Main's an egomaniac. This business of calling himself King of the Desert illustrates what I mean. He's sane, but at the same time his brain is twisted by illusions of grandeur."

"Mullins is plenty ordinary," Clay said. "I'll go out of that door before dark."

"Oh, hell!" Akin said wearily. "You're ordinary enough to die, too."

Clay dropped his cigarette stub on the floor and stepped on it. "How'd you happen to get nailed in the first place?"

"My mistake was coming into the desert. I'd been warned. Even Vicky told me I shouldn't come alone, so I lied to her, saying I was just going to Lava City. I kept going till I was halfway to Burns. One night Taber and Main rode into my camp and said I was coming with them. I tried for my gun like a fool, and Taber shot me. When I came to, I was in this room."

"Why didn't Main beef you?"

"He had the notion I could stop my company by writing a letter saying the physical difficulties were too great to warrant building across the desert. Main even wrote the letter and tried to make me copy it." Akin drew his shoulders back, his thin gray face reflecting the pride that was in him. "I refused, Bond. They starved me and they beat me, but I never copied that letter."

He had a right to be proud, Clay thought; and for the first time he understood why Vicky and Walt Paddon felt as they did about George Akin. He nodded. "It took guts."

Akin's shoulders went slack. "I—I was very close to surrendering when you came. Main knew that eventually time would do the job." Akin rubbed his face. "You know, I guess it was Vicky who kept me from giving up. I felt that there was no use living if I disappointed her."

"Funny," Clay said thoughtfully. "Vicky is loco about a railroad. I just don't savvy that."

"It isn't funny if you know her like I do," Akin said. "You see, she's sort of gaunted by the things her father did which according to her lights were wrong. She never said it just this way, but I believe that when the railroad is built she'll be a free woman." He spread his hands as if not quite sure he understood it himself. "I think she feels that she owes humanity a debt, and a big thing like a railroad would square it. Did you ever feel that way, Bond?"

"No, I never did."

"Then why did you come here?"

"To keep Vicky from coming."

Akin rose and walked to the window. "You love her. You know, Bond, you're a tough man. I never knew you before you met Vicky, but I have a feeling that you wouldn't have done this unless you had met her."

"Of course not. What are you getting at?"

"Just this, my friend. You'll help build this railroad, not because you want it or because Sid Starr killed your father or even because you sold the right of way to Paddon. You'll help because you love Vicky. It proves a principle I have always believed in, and I suppose it sounds funny coming from a tough old rooster like me. I've been tough enough in my day, too—don't you ever doubt that; but I've always believed that love is the greatest building force on this earth."

Akin walked to the door and jerked it open. He said, "Mullins, before dark Bond and I are walking through this door. If you try to stop us, you'll be a dead man."

Mullins's mouth sagged open in astonishment. "The hell! Just try it, old man, just try it."

"We will, Mullins. That's a promise." Akin shut the door and came back to stand beside Clay. "Now he'll start to worry. He'll tell himself he has nothing to worry over, but he'll still worry."

"And his nerves will get tighter'n the strings of a bull fiddle." Clay laughed. "You know, Akin, I think we'll make a pretty good team."

"Yes, I'm sure we will. Many's the time I could have used a man like you." Akin motioned to the door. "Do you have an idea?"

Clay nodded. "After while when he's ripe for the plucking, you jerk that window up and holler at me to be careful when I go down. He'll come tearing in here, and I'll lay one on his chin."

"It will work, I think," Akin said, "but after that it will be up to you. Now I'll take a nap. I'm tired."

He lay down on the bed and dropped at once into a troubled sleep as Clay watched. In appearance he was much like Walt Paddon except that he was older. The difference was that, although Paddon seemed frail, actually he was as tough as the steel that goes into the mainspring of a watch. In Akin the physical weakness was no disguise. His age, the wound he had suffered, and the starvation diet Main had kept him on had taken their toll.

Clay sank into a chair and rolled a smoke. He had talked big to bolster Akin's courage, but he knew he was licked. It was quite possible he could get out of the room, for he judged that Red Mullins was no mental giant; but that was as far as he and Akin would go. If he were alone, it might be different, but he couldn't leave Akin, and the old man could not stand the strain of flight even if they were able to reach horses.

Akin slept on, his breathing now barely audible. Clay finished a smoke and rolled another, time a drag to him. The sun was noon-high and was starting to drop westward. He began to feel the pangs of hunger and wondered if Main intended to starve them.

Suddenly Main's great voice hammered against his ears. "Light and rest your saddles. Time for dinner."

Clay's first thought was that the sheriff had come. He ran to the window and looked down into the dusty yard. For a moment he could not think and he could not breathe. Vicky and Jason Wade had ridden up and dismounted. Now they were walking toward the house.

Chapter Twenty-One: THE FRIENDLY MR. MAIN

CLAY'S FIRST EMOTION was anger. He had told Saul Benton to keep Vicky at the roadhouse, but here she was, walking into Bronc Main's house as calmly as if she were making a social call. Then the anger left him. He wheeled to the bed and shook Akin. "Wake up! Wake up!"

Akin stirred and shook his head. Still foggy from sleep, he asked petulantly, "What's the matter with you?"

"We're going through that door now. Vicky just rode in with Jason Wade."

The words knocked the sleep out of Akin as effectively as a bucket of cold water. He sat up and came onto his feet. "I should have known she'd do that." He started toward the window. "Get over to the door, Bond."

"Wait a minute. I've got a better idea."

Clay grabbed the chair and reached the door in three strides. He swung the chair against the wall, a shattering blow that reduced it to kindling, and snatched up a leg just as the door slammed open and Mullins rushed in, a cocked gun in his right hand, bawling, "What the hell do you think—" Clay brought the chair leg across his head in a short brutal blow that sent him sprawling.

"Sounded like you busted a watermelon," Akin said, pleased. "That kind of evens up for some of the beatings he gave me."

Clay snatched up Mullins's gun and wheeled toward the door, calling, "Come on."

On any other occasion Clay would have moved with more caution, but now he rushed down the stairs, boot heels cracking on the steps, Akin behind him. He had no definite plan, only a vague idea that he could hold his gun on Main while Vicky rode away. He reached the hall at the foot of the stairs and came to a flat-footed stop, for the cook stood there in the gloom, a double-barreled shotgun in his hand.

"Thought you had the bit in your teeth, didn't you?" Squint asked complacently. "Well, you ain't running far, bucko, not far. Now you can drop Red's gun unless you want a sample of my buckshot."

Akin stood beside Clay, both momentarily frozen as they stared at the cook. For a moment there was no sound except their heavy breathing; then they heard Main say, "It's a real pleasure to have you here, Vicky. And you, Jason. Yes, sir, a real pleasure."

"Come on, come on," Squint said impatiently, jerking his head toward the front room. "Drop that gun, Bond, and get in there. You're gonna make me late with dinner."

Clay obeyed, the heavy gun clattering to the floor. He moved along the hall, Akin in step beside him. When they came into the front room Main asked as if astonished, "Why, Squint, what's the scatter-gun for?"

"It means Red Mullins ain't smart enough to work for you," Squint said in disgust. "I told you that—"

"What'd he do?"

"I dunno. But I made a damned good guess that Bond would try to bust out when he saw the girl ride up, and likewise I guessed that he'd outsmart Mullins, so I grabbed the scatter-gun and waited for 'em at the foot of the stairs." Squint motioned toward Clay, his good blue eye filled with triumph. "Here you are, Bronc. If I hadn't nailed him, you might have had some trouble for yourself."

Vicky stood just inside the door, her head held high, the sunlight on her back. She gave Clay a quick glance when he came into the room, then her gaze swung to Akin. "Are you all right, George?"

"Sure," Akin answered, "but what are you—"

"You're awfully thin, George," Vicky said. "Hasn't Main been feeding you?"

"Not much." Akin threw out a hand in an angry motion toward Main. "You've had your fun with us. Let the girl go."

"You've got things mixed up, George," Main said mildly. "I'm not keeping any of you. You'll all be riding out of here soon as we have dinner. Fact is, I don't want you around here." He moved past Clay and took the shotgun from Squint. "Hurry the grub up, Squint. I expect these people want to start back to Lava City."

The cook's mouth sagged open, his good eye filled with amazement, his brown glass one staring absently into space. "You ain't letting—"

"Get to hell out of here," Main bawled. "Get that grub on the table, damn it. Of course I'm letting 'em."

Squint fled as Main laid the shotgun across the crude table in the middle of the room. Clay, watching the big man, sensed that this whole thing was as phony as a tent show. He had expected Main to go into a violent rage when Squint pushed the two of them into the room; he had expected to feel Main's battering fist or, at best, to be ushered back up the stairs. Instead, he was smiling affably, his wide, red-veined face thoroughly at ease.

"I'm sorry about all this, ma'am," Main said. "I expect you and Jason are mighty hungry. Nothing like desert air to give a person an appetite. Now just sit down." He motioned toward a bench by the door. "Sometimes I think I'll have to get a new cook. Squint is always getting his nose into business that ain't rightfully his."

"I said all the time that everything would turn out all right," Wade cried. "It was Bond who made all the trouble. He killed Taber, Bronc. Vicky and I had nothing to do with it, but Bond—"

"That's all right, Jason." Main motioned toward the bench again. "Sit down, you and Vicky. I know my friends, and I figure you're among them. Wouldn't even surprise me if you've decided a railroad was a bad thing for the country."

"Sure," Wade agreed eagerly. "At least the Oregon Southern would be a bad thing. I respect Hugh Kyle—"

Main boomed out a laugh. "So you respect my friend

Kyle. Well, sir, I don't, and I don't respect you. So dry up. Bond here has got his share of guts, and Vicky has kicked up her share of dust right along. Even old man Akin has stuck to his guns; but you're just a pussyfooting, easy-talking dude who should have stayed in town. Now sit down and shut your mug."

Wade dropped down on the bench, his face red, his hand trembling.

Clay said, "That's the first honest thing you've said since Squint shoved me in here. Let's have it straight now."

Main sat down on the table and leaned back, big hands clasped over one knee. "All right, I'll give it to you straight. This ain't all love and roses as you know damned well; but I'm fixing to turn you loose. I don't have to. You savvy that. It's just that I'm getting tired of all this ruckusing. I'm ready to make a deal." He nodded at Akin. "How about it, old man?"

"No deal," Vicky said sharply.

"We'd better listen, Vicky," Clay said. "If you'd stayed out of this like I told you, it would have been different. Now you're here, and that gives Main a pat hand."

She sat down, flushing. "I couldn't stay out of this, Clay. You ought to know that."

"I don't know anything of the kind," he said irritably. "What do you think I bought into this for?"

"Let's do our feuding some other time." Akin crossed the room and dropped wearily to the bench beside Vicky. "Clay's right. You shouldn't be here; but you are, and we must accept the hard and irrevocable fact that Main is a thief and a killer who recognizes no law. Whatever he does will be to his advantage." He nodded at Main. "Let's hear your offer."

Main was obviously enjoying the situation. His heavy lips were parted; his tiny eyes glittered with malicious satisfaction. Now he leaned forward, one meaty hand coming up to stroke his bushy mustache. "I ain't as low-down as you're making me out, Akin. Sure, my man shot you, but you was brought in and taken care of and fed. You owe me your life, and you're downright ungrateful."

"Oh, hell!" Akin cried. "You shot me, and then you damned near starved me to death. You beat me trying to make me sign that letter you made up. Nothing's changed except that Vicky played into your hand by coming here. Now let's get down to cases."

"That's what I aim to do." Main slid off the table and walked across the room to a shelf, lifted the lid of a cigar box, and took a cigar. "I'm a cattleman, and I aim to stay a cattleman. The desert ain't fit for farming, and what the office boys back in Washington say don't change nothing."

There was, Clay knew, a great deal of truth in this, and another man than Main could have made a case for himself. The real cause of the trouble lay in his character, in his attitude toward law, in the methods he had chosen to defend his range. It was totally unlike him to offer a compromise as long as he held the whip hand, so that his conciliatory attitude stemmed either from a knowledge that he actually didn't hold the whip hand, or from a sadistic pleasure in playing cat-and-mouse with them.

Main fired his cigar, gaze moving from one to the other. He went on. "I said I was fixing to turn you loose, and that's what I'll do as soon as we eat. There's just one catch, Akin. You could go to the sheriff, and swear out a warrant for me. You could charge me with attempted murder and kidnaping, and it might go a little rough with me." He tilted back his head and blew out a plume of smoke. "I ain't fooling myself. There's some folks in the county seat who would like to see me whittled down."

"You want me to promise I won't prefer charges," Akin said. "That it?"

"That's it, old man. I'm swapping your lives for a promise. That's fair, ain't it?"

There was a silence a moment, a strained silence as Clay, Akin, and Vicky considered the offer. Wade sat with his head down, hands clasped in front of him, a beaten man whose pride had been utterly stripped from him.

"Cash Taber said almost the same thing," Vicky said. "Maybe Main's on the level."

"It ain't in Main to be on the level," Clay said irritably.

Main wheeled on him, the familiar brutality tightening the coarse features of his face. "You're in a hell of a shape to say that, mister. You can take my deal or leave it."

"We'll take it," Clay said.

"Now wait a minute," Akin cried. "I'm the fellow they shot and starved and beat. I want to see Bronc Main behind bars."

"So do I," Clay said, "but we won't put him there by sitting here."

"If you're just thinking of me—" Vicky began.

"I'm thinking of all of us," Clay cut in. "Likewise I'm thinking of a railroad we've got to build."

She gave him a quick smile that might have said she was convinced that he had come to believe in the things she did. She turned to Akin, the smile fading. "Clay's right, George. We can't bargain."

"Main wouldn't give a man dying of thirst a drink unless it paid him to do it," Akin burst out. "He wouldn't be making an offer at all unless he knows his position is weak. I say to play it out."

"Play and be damned," Main growled. "Sure it's to my advantage for you to walk out of here. I'll tell you why. Mulehide Cotter's got the sheriff on my tail for stealing Triangle S beef. I don't want you found in case he rides in, which same I figure he'll do before sundown."

"You see, Clay?" Akin cried.

Clay shook his head. "Use your head. If the sheriff does

ride in and they have a tussle, what happens?"

"We're hostages," Vicky said tonelessly.

"But it means he's licked," Akin said doggedly. "He won't ride out of the country and leave his outfit, and he don't want to fight the sheriff. We've got him boxed."

"He won't ride out and leave his outfit," Clay agreed, "so he'll stay here and fight. Chances are, he'll die right here, and we'll die with him."

Main was listening, the cigar tilted arrogantly between his teeth. He said, "You know, Akin, Bond's got more sense in his little finger than you've got in your head."

"How's getting us out of here going to help you with the sheriff's rustling charge?" Akin demanded.

"It won't, but I don't need help on that. He can't prove nothing. It'll just give him a reason to ride in and look around, and I don't want him finding you."

Akin took a deep breath. "All right, Main, I'll make the promise, but it won't keep a railroad off the desert if my company decides to build."

Main shrugged. "I ain't worrying about the railroad till it gets here." He moved to the door and called, "Lew, saddle the horses for our guests and one for you."

At that moment Main stood with his back to Clay. The shotgun lay on the table within twenty feet of where Clay stood. It could be a trap. One of Main's men might be watching outside the room with a gun in his hand, and the first move on Clay's part would bring a bullet; but it was his guess that they had bargained only for a few more hours of life, that it suited Main to have them killed somewhere in the desert instead of here in the ranch house.

He had that one short interval of time to consider his chances, then he made his play, hoping he could at least save Vicky's life. He lunged toward the table and had his hands on the shotgun when Main, making a half turn, drew his gun and lined it on Vicky.

"You want it this way, Bond?"

Main had made a remarkably fast draw for so large a man. Clay stepped back from the table. He said, "All right, Main."

"Now that's better." Main completed his turn as he holstered his gun. "I'm surprised at you, Bond. I hoped you wouldn't do that. We made a deal. Remember?"

Clay's head tipped forward, masking the disappointment that boiled through him. "Funny thing, Bronc. I forgot just for a minute."

"A bad memory gets a man killed awful easy," Main said reprovingly.

"So I've heard. What was that about Dagget saddling a horse for himself?"

"Oh, he's going to guide you to Lava City. You're going straight across the desert, and I was afraid you'd get lost."

"That's real thoughtful," Clay murmured.

"Sure, glad to do it," Main said heartily. "Now let's go put the feed bag on."

They moved toward the kitchen, Vicky falling into step with Clay. She whispered, "What does it mean, Clay?"

His eyes met hers; he saw the wild clawing for the right to hope that was in every nerve of her body, balancing the fatal intuition that told her Main had promised one thing while he meant quite another. There was no doubt in his mind now. Dagget's presence could mean but one thing.

He could not bring himself to tell her that death waited on the desert for them, so he said, "It means we're crawling out of a tight by the skin of our teeth."

Chapter Twenty-Two: THROUGH SAGE AND JUNIPER

IT WAS MIDAFTERNOON when they rode out of the Flying M yard, Akin and Wade in front, Vicky and Clay behind them, and Lew Dagget in the rear. There was a gun in his holster, a Winchester in the boot, and his battered face held an expression of pure sadistic triumph.

When they were fifty yards from the house, Dagget called, "We're heading southeast, Akin. Pull off the road. I don't know what kind of sweet talk Main gave you, but from here on I'm giving the orders. I'll kill the first one of you who gets out of line."

Clay hipped around in his saddle. "Main said you were gonna guide us to Lava City."

"Lava City, is it?" Dagget laughed. "Well, we're headed in the right direction, ain't we?"

Clay turned back, throwing Vicky a quick glance. She was staring straight ahead, her face set, dark-blue eyes smoldering with fury. She had lost, he thought, the last lingering hope that Bronc Main had any intention of keeping his word.

They rode steadily southeast across a long swell of the desert, through sage and rabbit brush and past an occasional juniper, twisted and bent by the shaping wind that whispered down from the shoulders of the high Cascades to roar on across the high desert. A pine-clad spur of the Blue Mountains rose to the north, the desert swept away to the south, marked here and there by barren rimrock, and directly ahead the Three Sisters and Broken Top made a serrated line against a bright sky.

The hectic days that lay between this moment and the night Clay had ridden into the yard of Benton's roadhouse stretched backward like so many years. He thought of the things that had happened during these crowded days and nights, of people and events that had shaped his sense of values and his hopes for the future; and most of all he thought how his indwelling sense of injury and hatred for the name Starr had been softened by his love for Vicky.

George Akin had said love was the greatest building force in the world. It was that, Clay thought, and more. It was an alleviative force, the magic soda that alone could sweeten the sour milk of life. He wanted to reach out and take Vicky's hand, to tell her how he felt, to erase that look of bitter despair by saying that they had a chance as long as he could move and talk and fight. But it was not the time. He had to take Dagget by surprise; and, in order to do that, he must let the man think they were stoically waiting the fate Bronc Main had planned for them.

Once Clay glanced back at the Flying M. There was a flurry of movement, of men saddling horses and mounting. Dagget said, "You're looking the wrong way, Bond." He brought a hand to his battered face, his yellow eyes darkened by the hatred an injured man feels for the one who injured him.

Shrugging, Clay turned his head. Jason Wade rode like a stuffed wool sack. Akin sat hunched forward, swaying a little, one hand clutching the saddle horn. He was keeping his seat by sheer tough courage, but he was too weak to last it out. Sooner or later he would tumble out of the saddle, and Clay wondered what Dagget would do then.

The strange business of Main pretending to be friendly was clear to Clay now. He simply wanted them to ride out as if they were free, to give the impression to anyone watching that they were under no restraint whatever.

Main had undoubtedly told the truth when he said he expected the sheriff to ride in and he didn't want Akin found. For weeks Vicky had nagged the sheriff with her suspicions, but he had refused to look for Akin because there had been no tangible evidence that a crime had been committed. Mulehide Cotter might have stumbled upon enough evidence to interest the sheriff, and a search for Triangle S hides might have turned up the fact that George Akin was being held.

Vicky's arrival had brought the whole thing to a focus. Main had hit on the idea of proposing a compromise that on the surface appeared reasonable, but it was Clay's guess that he had figured out a way to kill the lot of them without making it look like murder. He tried to put himself in Main's place, but he could not think like the Flying M owner; he could not stumble upon any clue that could lead his mind to Main's plan.

The sun dropped low above the mountains, and the air cooled within the hour. Akin was trembling, whether from the chill or from utter weariness Clay did not know; but he was sure that the railroad man was close to exhaustion. Vicky had been watching, and now she brought her eyes to Clay. She said in a low tone, "George is about finished. What will we do?"

"Nothing, I reckon, but I'll try." Clay hipped around in his saddle to look at Dagget. "How about a rest?"

"No rest," Dagget said. "We'll keep riding. Long ways to Lava City."

Clay turned back. "We'll go till Akin can't go no more. Then we'll see."

She nodded, understanding. "I wonder if Dagget killed Cooky. He would be capable of it."

Clay said nothing. There was nothing he could say that would be of any help to Vicky. All afternoon his mind had groped for some way to get at Dagget that offered promise, but he had failed. He had considered shouting to the others to scatter and ride fast, and had known at once it would be suicide. Dagget would prefer not to shoot them, but under those circumstances he would. Besides, Akin would be thrown the instant he brought his horse to a faster pace. There was nothing to do but play it out and hope.

The sun dipped lower toward the peaks; then they were close to a long hill known as Juniper Ridge, and the mountains were blotted from view. A notch showed directly ahead of them. Clay had never been here before, but he had heard of it, this Dry River Cut that had been made, or so he had heard when he was a boy, by an ancient stream that had drained the high desert in prehistoric days under a different climate.

The road between Lava City and Benton's roadhouse lay to the south, but there was a seldom traveled trail that ran through the cut. Clay stared at the boulder-strewn cliffs, and it struck him that this was the most natural spot in the desert for an ambush. There would be no need for guns. A single great boulder dislodged from either rim would start a slide that would cover anyone in the bottom under tons of earth and rock. It would be a literal case of the desert swallowing its victims.

They were near the first slope of Juniper Ridge and within fifty feet of the east end of the cut when Akin, without giving warning that he had reached the end of his endurance, slid sideways out of the saddle and hit the soft sandy ground as limp as a figure made of straw.

Vicky screamed as Akin's horse bolted. Dagget pulled his gun, yelling, "Let the old fool lie there. We're going on." Ignoring him, Clay pulled up and dismounted. He knelt beside Akin as the old man's eyelids flickered open.

Akin breathed, "Don't go into the cut."

He had faked the fall, Clay thought, although it was doubtful if he could have gone much farther. The knowledge that the two of them had made the same guess without consultation confirmed Clay's feeling that the guess was right.

Dagget rode up, his gun covering them. He said hoarsely, "Get back into your saddle, Bond. I tell you we're riding through."

"We ain't riding without Akin, and Akin can't ride," Clay said flatly. "I asked you while ago to take a rest, but you were too damned bullheaded. Now we can't go on."

"We'll go, or you'll stay here permanent," Dagget bawled. "I'm giving you ten seconds."

"I'll need a little more than that," Clay said. "I'm toting Akin over there to the cliff so he'll be out of the wind. Wade, fetch his horse in."

Wade had been motionless, showing no interest in what was happening. Shrugging, he reined his horse around and rode toward Akin's animal that had come to a stop some distance away and stood looking at them, ears up.

Ignoring the fuming Dagget, Clay picked up Akin's thin body and carried him through the sage to the south wall. It was low here, perhaps twenty feet high, but not far to the west it tilted up precipitously until it reached a height of five hundred feet or more.

Clay laid Akin down, and stripped his horse when Wade rode up with it. He eased the saddle under the old man's head, then covered him with the blanket.

"All right, all right," Dagget said. "You fixed him up nice and cozy. Let's get on to Lava City."

It was dusk now, purple shadows flowing out across the sage, the last bright glitter of sunlight touching a distant peak of the Blue Mountains. Clay glanced up at the dark rim above the cut. There was no sign of life, but the break was so sharp that a man would have to be leaning over to be seen.

Slowly he brought his eyes to the angry Dagget. "Lew, it strikes me as being damned queer, you hurrying like this to get to Lava City."

"I've got a poker date in the Red Crow," Dagget said sullenly. "We could get there in time if we kept moving."

"And leave Akin to die. No, I don't think we'll do that." Clay motioned to Wade. "Climb down, mister. We'll get a fire going. It's gonna be cold before long."

"I'll fetch your horse," Vicky said, and rode back for him.

Dagget brought his mount in close, the muzzle of his gun within three feet of Clay's head; but before he could speak a shot was fired from the north rim. He stiffened, surprised, and tilted his head to stare at the cliff. There was no other sound, and when he brought his eyes back he was plainly puzzled.

"Now who would that be?" Clay murmured.

"Dunno," Dagget said uneasily. "I'll help get that fire started."

His sudden change was unexpected and, as far as Clay could see, entirely illogical. They broke limbs from a dead juniper, and within a few minutes had a fire going beside the motionless Akin. He was conscious, his eyes wide, but he seemed to be in a stupor, or he was still faking. Clay was not sure which, but he knew, and he had a feeling Akin knew, that the moment Dagget thought the railroad man could ride he'd insist on going through the cut. If the hunch was right they would have a choice between dying under a rock slide, and dying before Lew Dagget's gun.

Akin muttered, "Water," and Clay brought his canteen. He took a drink and slumped back, eyes staring upward. Vicky knelt beside him, holding his hands, but it was doubtful that he was aware of the girl's presence.

Clay motioned to Wade and Dagget, and they went back to the junipers growing above the rim. Returning, they dumped armloads of wood beside the fire, Dagget saying, "We've got to have water, Bond."

"Benton's roadhouse ain't far," Clay said.

"We ain't going back," Dagget said doggedly. "Lava City's just about as close, and that's where we're headed."

"You aim to go through the cut?"

Dagget hesitated, eyes raised to the north rim. Then he said, "Yeah, through the cut."

Clay hunkered beside the fire and rolled a cigarette. He said, "We'll wait a little longer. If Akin gets rested, he might come out of it."

"We ain't waiting much longer," Dagget said ominously, and moved around Akin to the wall and stood with his back against it, watching Clay.

Wade, too, drifted away, and presently Vicky came to sit beside Clay. Darkness had moved in around them, and the night wind flowed through the cut and touched them with chill fingers. Overhead stars made a cold glittering brilliance across the sky. The desert lay all around them, vast and empty, without light and without life. It seemed to flow on and on endlessly as if neither time nor space could be measured in a land where even the season brought little change.

"George is asleep," Vicky said. "I think he's all right."

"Sure," Clay assured. "Just worn out. He must have been quite a man in his day, but he should have known he was too old for this."

"He's told me several times he was never one to sit behind a desk. He'd rather die on a job than just rust out."

"He's coming mighty close to getting what he wants," Clay said grimly.

"He just can't go on tonight, Clay. There must be something we can do."

Clay looked at her, the blue eyes that appeared black in the flickering firelight, the pliant mouth that seemed to have forgotten how to smile, and he thought how much this girl had changed his life. He reached out and took her hand, saying, "We will do something."

It was possible that Dagget heard him, for he came up now. He said, "We're riding."

Clay dropped Vicky's hand and turned his head to look up. The big man's gun was pointed at him, and in the fringe of firelight he caught the expression that was on

Dagget's face. There was worry and fear in it, but there was determination, too. He had waited as long as he would. It must have been the shot they had heard from the rim that had brought the worry, and the worry had been responsible for the additional time. Dagget had already waited longer than Clay had expected.

"What about Akin?" Clay asked.

"He'll ride or he'll stay here. Get on your feet, Bond."

From the time they had left the Flying M, Clay had known this moment would come. He had tried to think what he would do; but now the moment was here, and he still didn't know. Dagget was capable of shooting him where he sat. The others would ride with him or be shot. It was a case of certain death here, or taking a chance on riding through the cut. There was the possibility he had guessed wrong about the rock slide. Or, even if he had guessed right, there was the long chance they could ride fast enough to get safely through the cut.

"All right," Clay said. "That iron you're holding is downright convincing."

Clay had not seen or heard Jason Wade for several minutes. He had given the promoter little thought, for he expected nothing from the man; and apparently Dagget had discounted him in the same way, for he had not made certain of his position. It was a fatal mistake, for now Wade came lunging out of the darkness.

Clay had started to get up, but with the first hint of Wade's rush, he dropped flat in front of Dagget, yelling, "Look out, Vicky." She fell away from the fire as Dagget, acting instinctively, let go a shot at Clay that burned with white heat along his left collar bone.

Dagget had no other chance. Wade dived headlong into him, sending him reeling toward the fire. He squalled, tripped over Clay, and sprawled on his face at the edge of the flames, his gun falling from slack fingers.

Clay scooped up the dropped gun and rolled away as the big man scrambled to the other side of the fire, scattering coals and charred ends of juniper limbs. He came to his feet and whirled, slapping out glowing sparks on his shirt, and found himself staring into the muzzle of his own gun.

"I reckon we're ready to ride all right," Clay said tonelessly, "only you're riding in the lead this time."

Wade was back on his feet, shouting hysterically, "So I made a damned fool of myself, did I? Your boss says Bond and Vicky and Akin have got guts, but I'm just a pussy-footing, easy-talking dude who should have stayed in town. What do you think of me now, Dagget?"

Dagget began to curse him in a flat bitter voice. Clay said, "Shut up. I'll tell you what I think, Jason. You're a damned good man when the chips are down."

Akin stirred and sat up, blinking owlishly. Vicky came around the fire and touched Wade on the arm. "I'm sorry, Jason, about what I've said and thought about you. If we live, we'll owe our life to you."

"You won't live long," Dagget shouted. "Not long. You hear?"

"Climb into your saddle, Dagget," Clay said. "Wade, you and Vicky pull gear off your horse. Get Akin's, too. I hate like hell to do this, but I figure Main's bunch is sitting up there on the north rim waiting for us. We'll whip the horses up and send 'em through with Dagget. Then we'll see."

Chapter Twenty-Three: HUGH KYLE'S CONSCIENCE

HUGH KYLE TURNED to the mahogany after Clay Bond and Paddon left Clancy's Bar in Triumph. He fingered the bruise on the side of his face where Bond had struck him, and at that moment he hated him with all the passion of which he was capable. It had been a long time since anyone had struck him. That in itself was enough to injure his pride; but worse was the fact that he had lain on the floor and stared up at Bond's angry face. He had simply lacked the will to get up and fight, and now he was ashamed.

He was alone in the saloon with the bartender. He motioned for a drink. The barman poured it and stepped away. He moved along the mahogany, industriously mopping it while he covertly eyed Kyle.

Wondering who I am that I wouldn't fight Bond, Kyle thought as his self-hatred grew. Then he began to rationalize. *The company isn't paying me to fight. Besides, I wouldn't have had a chance against Bond. I saw him lick hell out of Dagget.*

This thinking satisfied him. He poured another drink, suddenly content. It was not his way to feel strongly about anything or anyone for a long period of time, but he knew he was desperately tired of primitive living and the constant pressure of danger and the endless scheming to outmaneuver his opposition.

This was his last job out here. All he had to do was to block the Oregon Southern. He could do that. He wasn't sure how, and so far his luck had been bad, but he'd think of a way. Or if he didn't it was a good gamble that Main would do it for him. He didn't like Main's methods, but it had come to the place where almost any method that worked would be acceptable.

Kyle was not aware that Paddon had come back into the saloon until the Oregon Southern man said, "There's an old saying, Hugh, that when you rub up against a skunk, you get his smell on you."

He turned to Paddon, masking his face against the startled surprise that the words brought to him. "I hadn't heard that old saying, Walt."

"Just made it up," Paddon said. "I thought it was appropriate."

"Meaning what?"

"Meaning what I said while ago. I never figured you were the kind who'd get tied up with coyotes like Dagget and Main."

"I told you I didn't know——"

"All right, all right," Paddon said testily. "I won't say you're lying, but there's one thing you can't deny. The minute you hit this country, you got in touch with Bronc Main; and you've been in cahoots with him ever since."

"No crime in that. It's natural enough for two men who want the same thing to work together; but that doesn't mean I wanted Main or Dagget to murder anyone."

Paddon tapped the bar top. "Listen to me, Hugh. Listen good. You've got a fair to middling reputation in your home office. You wouldn't want to lose it, but, so help me Hannah, I'll bust it myself if you don't stop Main."

Kyle bristled. "My reputation in the home office is one thing you'd better leave alone. I've spent half a lifetime building it, and——"

"And it don't take long to lose it." Paddon shook his head. "We've had plenty of fights, you and me, but I've always kind of liked you. You look like the sort of man who'd build a railroad, and likewise you've got the look of a man who'd fit into a new country; but you're a fake, Hugh. The trouble is, you haven't got a heart."

"My organs are my business." Kyle scratched his chin, studying Paddon. "What makes you think I'll stop Main?"

"If he isn't stopped, he'll murder Akin. Vicky will go out to the Flying M, and Bond just left to find Vicky. That adds up to three lives you're responsible for."

"You said I didn't have a heart. Why should I worry about them?"

"It means your job. That's why. You and me will stoop

to any trick or legal shenanigan we can think of to stop each other. We'll wrangle in court, and we'll use money where it will do the most good, and we'll cuss each other with every word we know." He tapped a forefinger against Kyle's vest. "But not once have we attempted to kill a man. Maybe you don't give a damn about Vicky or Bond, but George Akin's life should be sacred to you."

"I haven't got anything to do with his killing," Kyle cried. "Why are you trying to pin it on me?"

"Because I want his life saved, and I think you can do it. If you don't, I'll promise that your company will hear the story, and you'll have a hell of a time proving that you didn't have a hand in Akin's killing."

For the first time in years real fear was in Hugh Kyle. Not physical fear, but fear for his future. The job he'd wanted for so long was within his reach, and Paddon could destroy his chance for it. There were some rules in a railroad war, and they didn't permit murder. It wouldn't be so bad if it was anyone but George Akin; but Akin was big in the railroad world, big enough to be respected even by his enemies.

"I can't guarantee I can handle Main," Kyle said, "but I'll try."

"It had better be a damned good try," Paddon said harshly. "There must be something big in this scrap I don't savvy, or you wouldn't have strung along with Main like this. It isn't like you, Hugh."

There was more to this than Paddon knew, but he wouldn't understand if he was told, for he was the sort who liked the job he had. Kyle took another drink, letting time ribbon out before he said, "I aim to block you, Walt. If I can't do that, I'll buy a right of way parallel to yours. Those are my orders, and I'll carry them out, come hell or high water; but I'll admit I made a mistake throwing in with Main. I'll do what I can for Akin."   ·

"What are you going to do?"

"Start riding. But the high desert's a big country. It may take a long time to find Main."

Kyle spun on his heel and left the saloon. Ten minutes later he was riding south, his mind filled with a seething turbulence. He carried a gun in a shoulder holster under his corduroy coat, and he knew he would have to use it. He had no illusions about Bronc Main. A gun was the only thing that would convince him he was wrong. He would not be touched by threats or appeals to logic.

Even now, filled with an uneasiness that was unusual for him, Kyle's precisionlike mind threaded its way through a maze of possible plans until it brought him to one that held some promise. He would find Main and go with him to the Flying M, saying he wanted to talk to Akin. After that his course would be determined by what Main did. He would use his gun when and if he saw a chance to get out alive with Akin.

He was not morally opposed to murder. It was simply a proposition that murder usually made life dangerous for the murderer; but it would be different with Main. There were a great many people in this country including the sheriff who would look upon Main's killing much as they would look upon the removal of a grizzly bear or a mad dog.

He swung off the road and angled southeast toward Prineville. Main might be hard to find, but the logical thing would be to look first in Prineville, then in Lava City. After that he would go to the Flying M; but it would be better if he could find Main first and ride along with him, pretending for a time that they were still allies.

Again an inner peace came to Kyle now that he had decided what to do, and his mind began to turn this situation to his own advantage. Personally he considered sentiment as a weakness, and he never felt that he was in debt to anyone because he had received a favor. That gave him an advantage over Akin and Vicky and Bond. Once he had freed Akin, he would be in position to ask a favor. If he couldn't block the Oregon Southern, he could at least persuade Vicky to let him have a right of way across her land; and if Bond remained stubborn she could work on him.

It was evening when he reached Prineville; but Main was not in town, and no one seemed to know where he was. The next day Kyle's luck was no better in Lava City. Inquiries at Royden's stable and the Red Crow and Old Peter Delong's store gained nothing except the news that Cash Taber had been in town and had left with Vicky Starr and Jason Wade.

The satisfaction that had been in Kyle began to wither. He had been certain he would find Main in one of the two towns. To go back to the Flying M at such a time was like retiring from battle, a thing Bronc Main would never do.

Kyle pondered this as he jogged through the junipers. He could find no explanation beyond the possibility that Main wanted to be at the ranch when Taber rode in with Vicky and Wade. Still, that did not seem entirely reasonable, for it was a situation Cash Taber would have no trouble handling.

By the middle of the day he discovered he was lost. Old Peter Delong had advised him to take the road and turn north beyond Benton's place, but Kyle had insisted he could find the Flying M by cutting across country. He had listened carefully while Old Peter told him how to get there, but he'd missed somewhere.

An hour after crossing Juniper Ridge he had lost his sense of direction. He found himself in a maze of hills and gullies that looked exactly alike, and it was evening before he knew where he was. Then he swore long and fer-

vently as he realized he had been riding in circles and had
wasted most of the day. He was back on Juniper Ridge.

The realization that he should have taken Old Peter's
advice produced a state of mental sourness. He never liked
to admit a mistake. His canteen was empty, he was hungry, and his horse was tired. He reined up, studying the
desert to the east. Benton's roadhouse was out there somewhere, and the road that would take him there lay to the
south. He turned that way, but before he had gone a mile
he came suddenly and unexpectedly upon the Dry River
Cut.

Anger grew in Kyle as he swung east again. There was
no crossing the cut at this place, and the distance to the
roadhouse was an uncertainty that gnawed at his mind.
He knew now that he had little chance of finding the road
before dark; and if he didn't find it he would have no
shelter for the night.

Half an hour later he felt a new surge of confidence.
Luck had swung his way again. There were three horses
directly ahead of him, and when he came closer, he saw
that the riders were hunkered close to the rim, and quick
exultation filled him with its warm glow. The man in the
middle was Bronc Main. Kyle waved a hand and brought
his tired horse to a faster pace. He might not have shelter
tonight, but at least he'd have a meal.

Main moved toward him, motioning for the others to
stay back. Kyle reined up and dismounted, saying, "Sure
glad to see you, Bronc. I left Lava City this morning and
planned to be at the Flying M a long time ago, but I got
lost."

He stopped. There was something dour and forbidding
about the big man. Main had called no greeting; he stood
spread-legged, his hands at his side. Now he said, his tone
hostile, "What would you be riding to the Flying M for?"

The light was thin, too thin to see his expression clear-

ly, but Kyle didn't need to see it. He realized he had made
another mistake, and this was a bad one. Main had often
called himself King of the Desert. Now they were on the
desert where Main felt he did not have to abide by any
law but his own will.

"What the hell's the matter with you, Bronc?" Kyle
demanded. "You act like we're not friends."

"We ain't, railroader. I've got a hunch you're out here
to see what kind of a grade your damned steel will have
to make crossing the desert. I told you once, and now I'll
tell you again. I won't have no railroad crossing the desert,
and that means either the Oregon Southern or the Columbia & Cascade."

"I came out to see Akin," Kyle said quickly. "I don't
care anything about laying steel across your desert."

"You're lying, but it don't make no difference." Main
motioned toward the cut. "Akin will be coming through
now any time, along with Wade and Bond and Vicky
Starr. We're fixing to bury 'em under a million tons of
rock."

The first thought that ran through Kyle's mind was
that he had to save Akin's life even if it meant killing
Main. He heard his own horrified voice beating against
his ears. "That's murder, Bronc. You can't do it."

Main laughed. "Yep, reckon it is, but you taught me
something the other day in the hotel in Lava City. You
said that the long way around was the best. That's the
way I'm taking. I could have shot the lot of 'em at the
Flying M, but sometimes bodies are found on the desert
no matter how good you hide 'em. This way they won't
be. Or if they are, there won't be no bullet holes in 'em."

One frantic thought pursued another through Kyle's
mind. The job that waited for him if he succeeded here!
Paddon's threat! The necessity of saving Akin's life! He
shouted through dry lips, "I won't let you, Bronc. It's

crazy. I won't let you."

"Got a conscience, have you?" Main's laugh was an unpleasant sound that mocked Kyle. "That's damned hard to believe."

Kyle was remembering that when Bond had knocked him down he had lain motionless on the saloon floor. He had been afraid to fight. But he wasn't afraid now. He would not dodge this and live with his shame again.

He started to run toward Main, right hand digging for his gun. He had to kill Main to save Akin to save his job— His gun was out. Bronc Main stood before him, too big a target to miss. But he didn't squeeze the trigger. Main's shot slammed out into the stillness; there was a single ribbon of flame leaping into the twilight, and Hugh Kyle started to fall. He kept falling, and then all sight and sound were lost to him and he lay on his face in the loose sandy soil.

Main stirred his body with a toe. "I didn't think he had the guts to draw on me," he said slowly as if he found it hard to believe. He swung back to his men. "Toss him over the rim, Mullins. Might as well bury him along with the rest of 'em."

Chapter Twenty-Four: THE KING IS DEAD

THE EARLY-MORNING AIR was thin and chill and sharply fragrant with mountain smells as Clay and Vicky rode into Lava City. The town still slept, the only sounds that of a man chopping wood behind the hotel and the clarion crow of Old Peter Delong's rooster.

There had been little talk on the way in. Both Clay and Vicky would carry in their minds for a long time the memory of the thundering rock slide that had seemed to shake the earth. It was a terrible thing that could have been spawned only in the mind of a man like Bronc Main.

The way Clay saw it, Lew Dagget's death was no trag-
edy, for he had died the way he had planned for Vicky
and Akin and Clay to die. Jason Wade, too, but that had
been incidental. He had simply been along; he had been
discounted by all of them, yet he had come up out of the
valley of shame to risk his life in an effort to save the
others. At the time he had not realized what lay ahead for
them. To some men the heroic comes easy, but Wade was
not one of those. As long as he lived, Clay would respect
Jason Wade.

Now, with the first cabins of Lava City on both sides
of them, Vicky asked, "What are you going to do, Clay?"

"I'll finish it if Main's in town. You'd better get over to
Royden's stable first thing and have him send a wagon
out for Akin and Wade."

"Of course, Clay." She paused, throwing him a questioning glance, then she asked, "You think Main's here?"

He nodded. "Just a hunch. He went to a lot of trouble
to get us and make it look like he didn't have anything to
do with it, so I've got a notion he lit a shuck for town and
he'll try to make folks think he's been here all night."

"But you can't fight his outfit, Clay."

"It'll be quite a chore," he admitted.

"I know the men in town. They're on our side because
they want a railroad, and none of them like Bronc Main.
They'll help if they know what has to be done."

"But how—"

"Let's see Old Peter Delong before you start looking
for Main."

He hesitated, having no great faith in the townsmen,
but he did respect Vicky's judgment. "All right. Won't
hurt nothing, I reckon."

They swung off Main Street and came in behind Old
Peter's store. He had living-quarters in the back, and as
they dismounted they heard the rattle of pans. "In time

for breakfast," Vicky said, and knocked.

Delong opened the door, and although he must have been surprised he gave no sign of it. "Come in, come in. You've had a fine night for riding."

He stepped aside, and they went in, Vicky saying, "We haven't been riding just for the fun of it, Old Peter."

Clay moved to the stove and held out his hands. "Tell him, Vicky."

The old man listened attentively while she told him what had happened. Then he said, "Before I went to bed, I saw some of the Flying M crew in town; but I cannot say whether Main is here or not. Walt Paddon is. I'm sure of that. Now I'll go over to the hotel and find out."

"I'll go along," Clay said. "All I want is some help to keep Main's boys off my neck."

"You'll have it," Old Peter said. "You said you were going to the livery stable, Vicky?"

"Yes."

"Tell Royden to come to the hotel. He has a kid working for him he can send with the wagon." Delong turned to the stove. "I'll finish breakfast and then we can—"

"Let's do the chore now," Clay said.

A smile touched the old man's lips. "I guess it would be better." He stood motionless as if wanting to say something, and then apparently decided against it, for he stepped into his bedroom and returned with a double-barreled shotgun. "I'm too old to shoot straight with a Winchester, but I can do some damage with this."

He led the way into the store and along the counter to the front door. He fumbled with the lock, turned it, and, opening the door, stepped into the street. He said to Vicky, "Hurry," and made the turn toward the hotel. Clay kept step beside him, and when Vicky was gone he said, "I remember your father very well, Clay, and I respected him. There were some qualities in Sid Starr that I could respect, too. He was a hard man, and he did not respect the law; but he was not, as some have said, the Bronc Main of his day."

Clay lifted his gun from leather, checked it, and eased it back. Then he turned to look at the old man, wondering what lay behind the talk. "I guess there wouldn't be another man quite like Bronc Main," he said.

"No, it is fortunate there is only one. It was different with your father and Sid Starr. Starr had something your father wanted; they were both too stubborn to compromise, so they had to carry their quarrel to its ultimate conclusion. It was wrong because it has brought trouble to both you and Vicky, but I have never been sure in my own mind that one was more to blame than the other."

They had reached the hotel, and Old Peter paused, a hand reaching out to grip Clay's arm. "It has come to me that you feel Sid was entirely to blame, and you still carry in your heart—"

"Forget it," Clay said impatiently. "I understand some things I didn't when I got back. Now let's get this over with."

"Good," Old Peter said. "I was afraid I would not have time to say this when it was over, but I see it does not need to be said." He smiled a little then. "You see, Clay, there are a great many of us who love Vicky in one way or another, but we are all alike in one way. We want her to be happy."

They went into the hotel. The clerk stirred in his chair behind the desk, yawned, and got up. He asked, "Ain't this a little early to be toting a shotgun—"

"Main here?" Clay cut in.

"Yeah, I think so. I ain't seen him, but one of his boys got rooms last night for the whole outfit. He said they were going to have a time for themselves, and Bronc and the rest would be along later. I was in and out till about two, but they came in all right. Keys were gone, anyhow."

It was the way Clay had thought Main would arrange it. He had an alibi of sorts—not an ironclad one, but one that would do. His men would swear that none of them had been near Dry River Cut, that Akin and his party had left the Flying M and they had not seen them since. If anyone discovered the slide and was suspicious and energetic enough to move a few tons of rocks, there would still be no proof that Main had been guilty of murder.

"How about this man?" Clay motioned to the clerk.

"He'll do." Old Peter patted his shotgun. "We've made our living from this country for a long time, Jake. Now we're paying back. I'll go get Paddon. Which room?"

"Twelve. What in hell are we—"

"We're keeping Main's boys off Bond's neck," Old Peter said.

"I'll be across the street when you get around to waking Main up," Clay said. "Tell him he's got a date with a ghost."

Old Peter nodded. "I'll tell him," he said, and turned up the stairs.

The clerk eyed Clay for a moment, then he said, "So it's finally come. Well, I hope you do the job or it'll be tough on the rest of us." He reached under the desk for a Colt. "But I'll sure back your play, mister. Main's overdue for a fall."

It was, Clay thought, almost exactly what Saul Benton had said that first night at the roadhouse. He left the hotel and crossed the street. When he reached the other side and turned back, he saw Royden come out of the stable and hurry along the walk to the hotel, a Winchester in his hand.

The seconds ticked away. Clay waited, loose-muscled. He could not see what was going on inside the hotel, but he had faith in Walt Paddon. If Old Peter Delong let him give the orders, the job would be done right.

The sun was up now, its brittle morning glare hard upon the street. Lava City was slowly waking. Someone coughed. The swamper in the Red Crow came out and heaved a bucket of dirty water into the street, and went back. Clay heard the rattle of a wagon behind the livery stable, and knew that the kid who worked for Royden was leaving town. Then Bronc Main came out of the hotel. He was alone.

At first sight of Main in Benton's roadhouse, Clay had underestimated him, thinking the man depended entirely on Cash Taber to do his fighting for him. That had been true; but now Taber was dead, and Bronc Main was not sidestepping the final showdown. If there was any cracking in his great faith in himself or his destiny, it did not show on his wide, red-veined face.

"Did you know you killed Lew Dagget last night?" Clay called.

Main stepped down from the walk, right hand splayed over gun butt. Ignoring the question, he said in a brittle tone, "The first time I saw you I said I'd teach you some manners if you stayed. Now I'll do it."

He took one more step and then pulled. It was a fast draw, faster than Clay had expected, and his gun made its thunder before Clay's did; but it was the wild shot of a man too intent on shaking out the first slug. Clay's bullet hit him in the chest before he could fire again. He went down, but he struggled to his hands and knees and tilted his gun upward again.

Clay started forward, firing as he walked, and Main, jarred by a second bullet, let go with a slug that kicked up dirt within a yard of Clay's feet. It was his last, for strength was gone from him. He dropped on his stomach and somehow managed to roll so that his eyes met Clay's when he came over.

"You'll never see your damned railroad cross the desert," Main whispered. "It's too tough for you and Akin and Paddon. Too tough for everybody but me. I licked it. No-body—else—ever—will."

Then Bronc Main died, little black eyes staring unsee-ingly upward at a bright, cloudless sky. Men came run-ning into the street, hair disheveled, most of them clad in underwear and pants. Clay turned away to watch the Fly-ing M hands as they were marched out of the hotel and along the street to the livery stable, Paddon and Old Peter Delong on one side of them, Royden and the hotel clerk on the other.

"Akin all right?" Paddon called.

"He'll be in town before dark," Clay answered.

Old Peter paused, eyes on Main's still body. He said, "Sagebrush Napoleon! Well, he didn't live long enough to go to Elba." Then he swung after the others.

Clay had not seen Vicky leave the stable, but he saw her now as she stepped into the store. He ran after her, not realizing he still held his gun until he reached the doorway. He threw it into the street and went on into the store, calling, "Vicky."

She stopped in front of the shelves that were loaded with bolts of cloth and turned to face him, her slim body poised as if uncertain whether she should stay or run. He came quickly to her and stood there looking down, and he thought of Old Peter saying, "There are a great many of us who love Vicky in one way or another, but we are all alike in one way. We want her to be happy."

For a moment he felt utterly inadequate. He wasn't sure he could make her happy, and she deserved so much; nor was he sure he could say the right things, now that the time was here. He had to try, and he sensed that he would never have another chance like this.

"You'll have your railroad," he blurted. "Main said it

would never be built across the desert, and maybe it won't; but it'll be built to Lava City."

She stiffened and seemed to draw away from him as she asked, "Is it important?"

It was the last thing he expected her to say, and he saw at once that he had said the wrong thing. He hurried on. "It took me awhile to get things straight in my head, but I savvy a lot of it now that I didn't when I got back. I—" He stopped and threw out his hands in a gesture of futility. "I'm not much good with words, Vicky, but I'm trying to tell you that what is past is past, and I want to forget it. Nobody else is important to me but you. I love you, and I'm asking you to marry me, and I'll try to make you happy—"

"Clay, Clay," she whispered, "you're awfully good with words. Those are the ones I've been waiting to hear."

It took a moment for him to grasp this thing she had told him, to understand that she had changed in her way as he had changed in his. To each of them loving the other was more important than all the railroads that would ever be built up the Deschutes or across the desert.

He put his arms around her, and she came to him, her lips eager for his. When he kissed her he had a glimpse of what it would be through the years ahead, peace and a fair life where his family and property would be safe from the searching fingers of men like Bronc Main, and the inner satisfaction that comes only from loving and the certainty of being loved. It was what he wanted; he had found it by coming home.

Later she drew her head back and smiled up at him, a hand coming to his cheek to caress it. Then she turned toward the shelves, her eyes searching them. She said, "You know, Clay, I've got to speak to Old Peter. He hasn't got a thing that will do for a wedding dress."

Wayne D. Overholser has won three Golden Spur awards from the Western Writers of America and has a long list of fine Western titles to his credit. He was born in Pomeroy, Washington, and attended the University of Montana, University of Oregon, and the University of Southern California before becoming a public school teacher and principal in various Oregon communities. He began writing for Western pulp magazines in 1936 and within a couple of years was a regular contributor to Street & Smith's *Western Story* and Fiction House's *Lariat Story Magazine*. *Buckaroo's Code* (1948) was his first Western novel and remains one of his best. In the 1950s and 1960s, having retired from academic work to concentrate on writing, he would publish as many as four books a year under his own name or a pseudonym, most prominently as Joseph Wayne. *The Bitter Night*, *The Lone Deputy*, and *The Violent Land* are among the finest of the early Overholser titles. He was asked by William MacLeod Raine, that dean among Western writers, to complete his last novel after Raine's death. Some of Overholser's most rewarding novels were actually collaborations with other Western writers: *Colorado Gold* with Chad Merriman and *Showdown at Stony Creek* with Lewis B. Patten. Overholser's Western novels, no matter under what name they have been published, are based on a solid knowledge of the history and customs of the American frontier West, particularly when set in his two favorite Western states, Oregon and Colorado. When it comes to his characters, he writes with skill, an uncommon sensitivity, and a consistently vivid and accurate vision of a way of life unique in human history.